Fade to Tomorrow

Fade to Tomorrow

Stephen Mertz

Five Star • Waterville, Maine

First Edition
First Printing: February 2004

Published in 2004 in conjunction with Tekno Books and Ed Gorman.

Set in 11 pt. Plantin by Ramona Watson.

Printed in the United States on permanent paper.

Library of Congress Cataloging-in-Publication Data

Mertz, Stephen, 1947–
    Fade to tomorrow / Stephen Mertz.—1st ed.
        p. cm.
        Contents: Fade to tomorrow—A hit for the new age—The death blues.
        ISBN 1-59414-106-1 (hc : alk. paper)
        1. Detective and mystery stories, American.   2. Private investigators—Missouri—Saint Louis—Fiction.   3. Saint Louis (Mo.)—Fiction.   4. Blind musicians—Fiction.
    I. Title.
    PS3613.E788F33 2004
        813′.6—dc22   2003064356

For Eagle Park Slim

"When I hear music I fear no danger, I see no foe. I am related to the earliest of times, and to the latest."

—Thoreau

TABLE OF CONTENTS

Fade to Tomorrow 9

A Hit for the New Age 193

The Death Blues 215

FADE TO TOMORROW

PROLOGUE

The yellow Chevy Cavalier turned north onto Mackenzie, its steel-belted radials crunching on the frozen snow.

This stretch of Mackenzie was a quiet neighborhood of small businesses. At this hour, the Cavalier had the street to itself. Suburban St. Louis slumbered in the dark of three a.m. It was January, and the night air was frigid.

The car traveled a half block, then turned right into a parking lot that bordered a low, oblong building. The Cavalier braked to a stop. The driver killed the engine and lights.

Two men got out. They wore identical knee-length leather slickers, unbuttoned. They did not slam the Cavalier's doors but eased them shut quietly. Their breath clouded in the subzero temperature.

The men were African American. One was a mountain of muscle, with a scarred face. The other was lithe, dapper.

They moved soundlessly to a metal door set midway in the otherwise blank front wall of the building. A 120-watt bulb burned over the door.

The big man reached up. He wore black leather gloves, and unscrewed the bulb with two twists. The length of the building was pitched into inky blackness. The smaller man held a key. There was a muted click and the door swung inward. The men stepped inside, closing the door after them.

They were in a carpeted corridor that extended the length of the building. The walls were oak paneled, the lighting muted. The dim throb of music came from further down the hallway.

They strode purposefully, shoulder to shoulder, in the direction of the music like a well-rehearsed team. The big man took the lead as they approached a door to the right, and they both withdrew weapons from under their slickers. The big man carried a silenced 9mm Beretta. The other held a slim Italian knife with a nine-inch folding blade, which he flicked open. They plunged through the doorway, the big man staying in the lead, his partner close on his heels.

They had entered the control room of an elaborate recording studio. The music was louder now. The building seemed to pulsate with the heavy beat. To their left, a plate glass window looked down on the recording area.

A gold-chained, jersey-wearing rapper stood in the studio beyond the glass. He wore earphones and was grinding and snapping out his arms and making gang signs to the facing studio wall while he rapped. His facial muscles were stretched taut, as he rhymed to the booming, previously recorded music.

The control room was carpeted and cozy. The smell of pot was in the air. Two futuristic chairs, fronting the main console, spun around at the abrupt interruption. Each chair was occupied by a white man who had been intent on the rapper in the studio.

One of the whites was a bodyguard, built like a wrestler. He came to his feet, grabbing beneath his jacket. The big intruder's Beretta snapped and a 9mm slug caught the bodyguard in the head, pitching him backward into the chair.

The man beside him, a recording engineer, stared dumbly down at the corpse, then back at the intruders.

The lithe, dapper intruder advanced toward him, his knife pointing forward at waist level.

12

The engineer stood up and stumbled back until the console stopped him. "No, wait. Please—"

"Relax. We've got no beef with you," said the big man.

The man with the knife paused six inches away from the engineer. "Turn around and forget. It'll just be a punch behind the ear. It won't hurt."

The engineer relaxed and turned.

The slim man slipped in close behind him and snaked a forearm across the engineer's throat, to hold him in place. With his other hand, he slid the knife in at the base of the engineer's spine, giving a twist with his wrist when the hilt sank against flesh. His lips quivered. He released his chokehold, withdrew the knife blade from the wound and watched the dead man fall to the floor.

Only seconds had elapsed. The music continued to boom. The rapper's voice blared through the studio's playback system.

The big man looked at his partner and nodded at the glass partition. "Give singing boy the news. I'll dust him."

The lithe man moved to the console, positioned directly below the window. He gazed out and for the first time he saw the woman in the studio.

A guest of the featured artist. Cool. Light chocolate skin. Stylish. She sat in the shadows, watching the man rap.

They were alone out there.

"Looks like we get a bonus this time, Spooner." The little man flicked a switch on the board and the music was cut off in mid-beat. The abrupt, complete silence startled both people in the recording room.

"Hey, what the hell, man?" The rapper's tone was peevish. "I had it close to nailed that time."

The man at the console thumbed another toggle switch that patched the control room mike into the sound system.

"Relax. You got more to worry about right now than some lame rap, Leon."

The rapper's expression changed. He tugged off his earphones. "I thought we was going to stay with my new name like on the CD. I'm Ice Crusher, ain't that right?" He squinted at the window of the control room, but could not see through it because of the reflected overhead lights in the studio. "Who's up there?" His tone grew surly. "Is that you, Jerry?"

"If Jerry's one of these white dudes, he's stone dead," said the man with the knife. "You're dead too, dog. Boss L, he don't like homes who cross him."

Leon's surliness began to fade, replaced by uncertainty. "I didn't cross nobody. Libra knows that."

"Libra, he thinks a big timer like you ought to be made an example of." Then, off-mike but with the microphone still switched on, the man said, "Okay, Spooner. Go out and cap him."

Leon/Ice Crusher heard that. He back-pedaled several steps as the connecting door from the control room opened.

Spooner came through, his Beretta in plain view.

The woman rose from the high stool upon which she'd been sitting. She stood beside Leon, their backs pressed against a soundproofed wall, their faces tight with fear.

"Now, hold on." Leon's voice cracked. "How much are you getting paid? I can double it, swear to God. I'll make it worth your while. Just let us go."

"Don't listen to him, Spooner," came the voice over the sound system. "Kill him quick, but save the ho. We'll have us some fun with her first."

Spooner pointed his Beretta almost nonchalantly at Leon. His eyes were already devouring the woman's figure. She wore revealing black.

Leon emitted a nervous laugh.

"Wait, I get it. This here is to scare me, right? Okay, okay. This boy done got the message. You tell Libra that I'll go along with—" Then, realizing that nothing he could say would change the fact that he was about to die, Ice Crusher's voice rose like a gospel singer's in church. *"No!"*

The Beretta snapped twice, two flat sounds in the acoustically perfect room, blasting the life out of Leon with ugly splat noises. He back-pedaled some more before crumpling to the floor, dead.

Spooner pocketed the pistol and started toward the woman, her body blocked from view of the man at the control room window. Her frenzied shriek pierced over the sound system.

The other man turned from the console and hurried to the doorway to the studio, balancing the long-bladed knife loosely in his hand. His eyes were bright.

CHAPTER ONE

Three months later . . .

Madison could tell instinctively that the first three human beings he had seen in more than a month meant trouble. He had just finished chopping wood, and was about to set out to check his traps.

Spring comes two or three times in the high country of western Colorado, when arid Chinook winds blow in from the southern desert. Heavy accumulations of snow vanish within days, leaving patches of muddy ground with daytime highs in the sixties beneath sunny, crisp blue skies.

The aromatic scent of pines on crisp high elevation air carried a nip strong enough to clear a man's head. His world was this cabin and these mountains; a pure, clean world hardly changed since time began.

He was thirty-two years of age, well-muscled, five-foot-ten, his hair too long to be stylish. He wore camouflage fatigues, and was armed with a short-barreled .44 Magnum revolver in a shoulder holster. A wide-bladed, double-edged hunting knife was sheathed at his left hip.

He had "retired" to his mountaintop following his honorable discharge from the military. He'd reached the rank of Colonel, and had served as an Army Ranger attached to the Central Intelligence Agency. He had worked countless "dirty ops" (secret operations) in hellholes from Afghanistan and Iraq to Colombia, from Somalia to Yugoslavia. But a man could only take so much blood and death, and so he had walked away. He had done his time in hell. He had paid his dues and learned what he could, and the time had come for a new phase of his life, which was this contemplative life on this mountaintop. These days, at least for the time being, he preferred his own company.

Once every few weeks Madison ventured down a winding, deeply rutted dirt road to a rural country store at the foot of his mountain, where he stocked up on necessary supplies. He had a generator and a solar setup but, for the most part, his lifestyle was that of a primitive mountain man, which was not uncommon in this country. Once you traveled beyond the town limits of any community out here, loners constituted a significant percentage of the scant population.

His concessions to modern living included a satellite dish and a radio antenna tall enough to be mistaken for a mountaintop weather station, and he owned hundreds of books and more than a thousand CD's that ranged from pop to rock to jazz to classical.

The land was bought and paid for, and so the world left him alone to mind his own business. There was only one thing that marred this idyllic life. He didn't much care for the work he had to take on—two or three jobs a year off in "the world" to pay for the way he lived . . .

His spread was ten miles north of Durango, in the southwestern portion of the state, nestled in the pines of the San Juan mountains, overlooking the cool green of the Animas Valley and the meandering Animas River. The air was clean, the people were healthy and sane, life was good; a life of close-to-nature days, and nights when the overhead panorama of stars became so clear and vast that you could not help but know that you were but a part of something majestic. This was a land where a person could find peace within one's own soul and within the universe in which we live.

He had been just starting out of the cabin when the buzzer had sounded stridently from across the room, stopping him in his tracks.

He crossed the interior of the one-room cabin to the electronic control panel, where he flicked off the alarm warning mechanism and activated the three closed-circuit television screens.

Three twelve-inch screens blinked and shimmered to life.

The center one picked up a rocketing, shiny new Buick Expedition, its windows heavily smoked, its bulk seeming to bounce effortlessly up the narrow, rutted, steep incline that climbed through the pine forest, just now crossing Madison's property line a half-mile southwest of the cabin.

No more than four or five minutes away.

He flicked off the system. He turned and drew down a Weatherby Mark V bolt-action .460 Magnum hunting rifle from its rack above the fireplace, then exited the cabin at a run. He didn't stop running until he reached high ground thirty yards from the cabin.

A few more months and he would have expected the occasional trespasser. Innocent backpackers, and not so innocent off-season hunters and poachers, would be venturing up his road, some of them driving as far as his cabin despite the clearly placed *No Hunting—No Trespassing* signs posted across his property.

These weren't hunters.

He positioned himself with his back pressed against the trunk of a towering pine, the Weatherby held perpendicular to his body. The sigh of a cool breeze through the pines and the earthy tang of nature enveloped him. He twisted around the tree trunk enough to peer down into the clearing in front of the cabin.

The van came to a heavily braked stop, rocking on its shocks. Three men debarked and stood near each other, but not clustered. Two of them held hunting rifles.

Madison recognized the one in the middle.

The one without a rifle. The man in charge. His name was Arn Shapiro. Middle-aged. A bear-like guy, balding, the remnants of his wiry hair worn on the eccentrically long, windblown side.

Shapiro lifted his hands to his mouth to magnify his voice, and shouted.

"Steve!"

Madison maintained his position. Ingrained, rising combat senses probed the thick woods in every direction for any sign of danger. The only such threat he could detect came from the trio down by his cabin.

He considered his options. Shapiro stopped calling his name. The three men stood gazing off in various directions at the forest that lined the ridges around the cabin. Madison noted that the two heavyset men with Shapiro held their rifles aimed at the ground, not in a firing position. And so he made his decision.

A hawk chose that moment to soar into the clearing, riding an air current high beneath the cobalt sky.

He slowly stepped from his concealment and assumed an easy gait, purposefully making himself visible to them as if he were approaching the cabin with no realization that they were there.

He had to remain visible for several moments longer than he'd intended because Shapiro chose that moment to gaze skyward, watching the hawk.

One of the men spotted him and shouted something that swung around the attention of Shapiro and the third man, which is what Madison was waiting for. He lunged back into the shadows at the base of the clustered pines.

Shapiro shouted something after him, but he couldn't discern the words. He heard nothing but their footfalls coming after him in hot pursuit along this rocky game trail that must have been here for a hundred years.

He poured on the steam, his legs pumping, and he came to a point where the trail dipped beneath a ridge in the terrain, taking him from his pursuer's line of vision. He jogged another fifty paces, then eased to his left, positioning himself behind another huge tree trunk that would effectively block him from their sight. He'd chosen and rigged this spot long ago, when he'd first gone about securing this hideaway.

They came over the ridge at a dead heat gallop, Shapiro in the middle, the rifle-toters evenly spaced to his either side. They topped the lip of the ridge, charging down the game trail, past where Madison knelt.

He waited until Shapiro was right where he wanted him, then leaned forward to sever a taut length of clear rope with one swift cut, springing the trap.

The loop of the nearly invisible line snapped around Shapiro's ankles while the tree limb it was attached to sprang up, tightening the loop into a knot around his ankles, whisking Shapiro upwards, upside down. He ended up with the top of his head three feet from the ground, dangling like bagged game ready to be skinned.

Madison stepped from his cover. He swung the Weatherby in an arc, like a club.

The man to Shapiro's right was turning around at the commotion of Shapiro being hoisted topsy-turvy, and he walked straight into the sharp smack of the rifle's ventilated, rubber recoil pad butt plate, which connected with his right temple. His knees buckled and he went down.

Madison pulled the Weatherby around into firing position on the third man, before the first had fully collapsed to the ground.

Shapiro swayed lazily back and forth like a human pendulum, cursing loudly, attempting to pull himself up and around. He reached up toward the knotted line around his ankles but could not bend himself back up far enough.

The third man had his rifle nearly around in target acquisition but ceased all movement like a robot with its juice cut off when he found himself looking into the Weatherby's muzzle. This one knows weapons, thought Madison. He'll know the Weatherby fires a 500-grain bullet that achieves one of the highest velocities of any bullet in the world. He'll know what that bullet would do to his chest if he made the slightest wrong move.

"Drop it." Madison spoke along the length of the rifle barrel. "You're Arn's bodyguard, but you boys are trespassing. The laws out here are kind of vague and happen to favor the landowner. What I'm saying is, I'll kill you and I'll get away with it. Now drop the rifle."

The man dropped his rifle.

Shapiro commenced flailing, trying to free himself without a chance of success.

"Damn you, Madison. Get me down from here, you crazy son of a bitch!"

"Shut up." Madison did not take his eyes or the Weatherby's muzzle from its bead on the third man. "Handgun, too."

He watched the man reach under his jacket and ever so gently remove a pistol from a concealed, shoulder holster. He held the pistol with his fingertips, away from his body, and let it drop to the ground.

An owl hooted from a nearby treetop.

Madison motioned with his rifle, directing the man to stand next to where the unconscious figure of his partner lay.

"Over there."

The man obeyed, hands raised, his mouth a tight, anxious gash.

Shapiro gave up struggling. Even in his predicament, he bristled.

"Jesus H! What the hell is this? Let me down, damn you. I come all this distance to offer you the biggest job I've ever offered you and this is the kind of a goddamn welcome I get."

Madison kept his peripheral vision on the man standing, and lowered the Weatherby so the muzzle nudged Shapiro's nostrils.

"You've still got your balls, Arn, I'll say that for you."

Upon his discharge from the service, Madison had encountered the dilemma common among demobilized combatants throughout history; namely, how to integrate his combat skills into civilian life. The CIA and several federal level law enforcement agencies had approached him, but his stint in the military had taught him that while he had the ability to both follow orders and command others, he retained scant taste for either. He was a disciplined free spirit. A combatant who appreciated the grace and beauty and power of art. He was an enigma to himself sometimes. He found employment with an L.A.-based security firm that supplied celebrities with bodyguards. His first assignment, traveling as security chief for a visiting British diva's night on the town, resulted in him shooting dead three people in a running firefight. Members of the singer's entourage had turned on her, bringing in professionals to stage a kidnapping. The singer was a worldwide superstar, and after that mess—

and his managing to keep even the scent of it from reaching the media—Madison's phone began ringing with offers.

Every supermarket tabloid provided ample proof on a weekly basis of the misfortunes that could befall entertainers who were worth millions of dollars.

Madison became a freelance "industrial consultant," of a sort, to the music industry. He was called in by promoters, by personal managers and music corporations, by movie studios, et cetera, whenever a valuable property—invariably a misguided artist in one of the performing arts—became enmeshed in a situation that could ruin a career and thereby cost said promoters, managers, et cetera millions and millions of dollars worldwide in future earnings.

At such critical times, when he accepted such an offer to intercede, Madison's only stipulation was the tacit understanding that he could employ any means necessary, which included extra-legal means on occasion, to extricate the stars in question from whatever tight spots they were in. Madison's job was to undo whatever damage had been done, and to accomplish this in a manner that avoided publicity.

Considering the sort kind of money they threw at him, he could afford to be selective in choosing his jobs, and took on usually no more than three or four per year. He'd been a garage band musician as a teenager. He was a terrible singer and guitarist although it was still a hobby, but he did share an empathy with every artist, with all of those souls afflicted with the bugaboo of self-expression.

A sensitive teenage poetess/songwriter had been found unconscious in her Montreal motel room during a tour, lying next to the brutally butchered body of a local newscaster. It was a frame-up, and Madison was called in to track down the real killer while managing to extricate the teenage singer from the situation; she'd been a victim in the frame-up too, and the authorities and the media never learned of her involvement in the case after the real killer was brought to justice, thanks to Madison's off-stage maneuverings. Another time, he'd tracked down the missing guitarist of the "bad boy" hard rock band on the eve of their world tour to promote their first album in four years. A fortune was riding on that tour. Several investors' fortunes, for that matter, and it almost didn't happen until Madison tracked down the Brit wastrel to his French chateau hideout and rescued him from the clutches of an ex-wife with hired goons and ideas.

For the past few years, Madison had found it lucrative enough to take on jobs solely from the man who now dangled before him.

Shapiro tried to maintain his composure, to sound smooth and persuasive, but it wasn't easy hanging upside down from a tree.

"Come on, Steve, cut me down from here so we can talk."

"Talk about the fifty grand you owe me for that Tokyo job."

Shapiro blinked. "Is that what this is about?"

"Stop it. You've got a job for me. You knew you'd catch some heat up here so you brought some protection along to impress me." He glanced at the bodyguards, one unconscious, and the other frozen in place. Some protection. "But yeah, Arn, this is about fifty thousand buckos. I don't like it when people owe me for my honest labor."

"You got your fifty grand per our agreement when the girls' plane touched down in San Francisco. That was three months ago!"

"You know what our agreement was. The Nicks Twins

got caught on an Asian tour in the wrong place with the wrong people, and the Tokyo cops were that close to busting the whole mess wide open."

"Musicians." Shapiro grumbled like an irritable bear. "Why'd I ever get into this business? Jesus, my ulcer."

Madison exerted the slightest pressure on the rifle muzzle, which further squished Arn's nose.

"We're losing focus here. You owe me fifty thousand dollars. Yeah, you paid me fifty. But it was fifty for each twin and the last I heard, those two nut cases were getting themselves nominated for three more Grammies."

"Steve, cut me down. We're supposed to behave like civilized people."

"Try behaving ethically," said Madison. "I'll say it again. You owe me fifty grand. It was a handshake deal between us like always."

"I can't leave any kind of trail on these things, Madison."

"Right, and that's okay. Cash works for me. I'm no fan of the IRS. But what's the deal this time? You're pushing some to see how far you can push, so you'll know how far to push in the future."

"Guess I'm learning, all right."

"I guess you are. Don't push me, Arn."

"Uh, I get the message." Shapiro's tone was nasal. "Damn, sport, the blood's running to my head and we've got heavy business to discuss. It was all a misunderstanding."

"You didn't return my calls. You didn't answer my e-mails. And you show up on my mountain talking misunderstanding and another job. Some balls, Arn. I want my money before anything else."

"And what will you do if I don't have the money? Blow my brains out?"

"I'm thinking about it."

"Christ, I believe he would. Okay, okay. Man! This is killing my back! All right, we'll use your computer. I can transfer the money from my account while you watch."

Madison stepped back, removing the end of the Weatherby's barrel from Shapiro's nose.

"Now you're talking."

His right hand flashed across his chest and the knife blade glinted for a second as it swept through the air in a downward arc. The length of line stringing Shapiro up was cut in two.

Shapiro plummeted headfirst to the ground, landing with a full-bodied *thump*.

Thirty minutes later, they sat at the table in the center of the cabin. Shapiro sipped from a glass of scotch while he nursed the bruise on his forehead with a makeshift ice pack.

The pair of bodyguards loitered out front of the cabin near their vehicle. The one man had regained consciousness, and both had been given their rifles back. Neither had concealed his open resentment of Madison when Shapiro had instructed them to wait outside.

Madison did not give much of a damn. He preferred a peaceful life. That's why he'd chosen a mountaintop as his home. But they had displayed weapons on private property—*his* private property—and they'd known the risks they were taking in working for a shark like Shapiro, or they should have.

Arn Shapiro was third generation music business. His father had booked sixties acts during the San Francisco hippie days. His grandfathers had immigrated with their families from the ghetto of Poland to the ghetto of America in 1938 to escape Hitler's ovens and had gone into the tavern business on Chicago's south side. Catering to this black inner city clientele, they had done well for themselves, and this had somehow led to the recording and local marketing of records by the blues shouters, guitar players, and boogie piano pounders who appeared at their nightclub. In 1955, a black rhythm and blues singer gave the Shapiro Brothers' small label its first national hit, and many more hits followed. The little company had gone on to become the largest independent in the business in its day.

Irv and Stan Shapiro were gone now, and so was their record company, swallowed up and ultimately discontinued by an oil company conglomerate during the late sixties. Arn's father was gone too, a drug overdose statistic of the 1970s. But thanks to Arn, the Shapiro name lived on in the music trade papers, and was every bit as powerful today as it had been in the days of Arn's father and uncle. In these days of MTV, handling stars big enough to cover every strata of the demographic map from hardcore rock and rap to the latest pop sensation *du jour,* Arn was the most powerful agent/producer/promoter in the history of global mass-market entertainment. In that arena's shark-infested waters, Shapiro was the biggest and baddest shark.

The PC in Madison's work alcove had been shut down after the transfer of funds to his account had been completed and confirmed. He was ready to talk business.

Shapiro asked, "What do you know about Johnny Willow?"

"Johnny is his generation's Stevie Wonder," said Madison. "He started cutting hit records when he was fourteen. At first, he was a novelty; the blind kid who looked and sounded like a cross between Stevie and Ray Charles, who seemed to master every instrument and techno innovation that came his way. Depending on which music critic you're reading, his lyrics are either spaced-out hippie, or paeans to enlightened planetary consciousness."

Arn snickered. "The way you talk."

"It's only what I've read. I like listening to his stuff. I program the up-tempo stuff on my headset CD player when I go skiing, and the dreamy stuff works for unwinding at the end of a day, with or without a woman."

"So you're a Johnny Willow fan."

Madison studied Shapiro, and tugged at an earlobe. "Okay. So that's who this visit's about. It's been two years since his last CD. That's a long time in the pop world, isn't it."

"Johnny's new CD was released today and he's promoting its release with a world tour, starting with a big comeback concert tonight in his hometown of St. Louis."

Shapiro shifted the ice pack over his bruise, and a trickle of water ran into his eye. He brushed at his eye with a sleeve.

"You're damned plugged in for a misanthropic mountain man."

"I've got a living to make."

"Do you know the real story behind this hiatus?"

"If there in a real story, in Johnny's world I'd say it was drugs. I remember considerable media coverage a year ago when his mother died. Johnny came from a tight family. His father was one of the greatest gospel singers of the fifties, right up there with Mahalia Jackson, and he's Johnny's personal manager. I read where Johnny was devastated when his mother died."

Shapiro's flat, glittering shark eyes clouded for a millisecond with what could have been sympathy. "That's when Johnny turned to smack. He'd been able to handle his blindness, racism, and the pressures of being a super star.

But after his mother passed, nothing Johnny's father did could keep Johnny from using the stuff."

"What's Johnny's current status?"

"Whistle clean. Has been for six months. I know. I was there. It was me, Johnny's dad, and Johnny's wife, Lana, who ganged up for an intervention just when Johnny was so sick from that junk, he was ready to die. We saw him through rehab."

Madison scrutinized Shapiro. He ran a thumbnail along his jawline.

"Damn, Arnold. I didn't know you had it in you."

"Don't call me Arnold. I was overseeing a business investment. Anyway, Johnny's had himself a rough year. But he was able to face and overcome what he was doing to himself, and he's a better man for it. And tomorrow night in St. Louis is supposed to be his night. You know how fast things happen in the pop world these days. My star will be an oldies act if he doesn't deliver big time. This will be the most important concert of Johnny Willow's personal and professional life."

"You said he's clean. What's the problem?"

Shapiro sighed. His eyes dropped to his whiskey glass.

"After he got out of rehab, Johnny and Lana took a vacation down to Jamaica. While they were down there, he got to know some of the hot local musicians and he absorbed the whole reggae thing minus the ganja. He cut his new CD down there. Then, about a month ago, he flew the guys in his new road band down to Kingston where they could pick up on the sounds and the feel of the place so they could even better understand what he was trying to do, and they held extensive rehearsals for this tour. There's a lot to get down. The music is complex; there's choreography and the laser show. Johnny's father accompanied the band to Jamaica,

29

and he told me that's where the trouble started."

"It's got to be drugs."

"Of course it is, but not with Johnny. Look, Steve, it's going down right *now,* as we speak. So I need to hire you right now. We're straight on the money so we're friends again, right?"

"Let's not get mushy. What are you hiring me to do?"

"Throw what you need into a bag quick and come with me and the boys in the Explorer. I've got one of my jets waiting at that rinky-dink airport up the road from town." Shapiro shook his head, and finished his drink with a pull. "Jeez, you're out here."

"If I fly to St. Louis, Arn, I fly alone."

Shapiro made a placating gesture.

"You think I don't know that?"

"I don't know. After that money shenanigan, you could be dumber than you look."

Shapiro pretended not to hear this.

"I'm flying with you as far as Denver. I'm co-producing a show there tonight and my partner likes to get funny with the money, so I . . . never mind. I'll be in St. Louis in time for Johnny's show. I guarantee you, Steve, nobody will cramp your style. So what do you say? You're in, right?"

"First," said Madison, "we talk money."

CHAPTER TWO

St. Louis, from the air by night, is beautiful.

Madison was well aware of the gritty reality of this "Gateway to the West." Nearly four million souls living, loving, hating, going to work, polluting, giving birth and killing each other, crowded into a sprawling old metropolis on the banks of the grimy Mississippi. The City of the Arch. Gateway to the West. An industrial city with the bleak ugliness that only an industrial city can have. A tough town by any standard.

But from the air at night, St. Louis is beautiful. Beyond the rain-streaked window beside Madison, a carpet of lights shimmered out to infinity beneath the Cessna as it banked in for its landing.

He was the only passenger. He wore faded denim, western boots, a black T-shirt and a black leather jacket. Concealed beneath his jacket was the short-barreled .44 Magnum, in a holster under his left arm.

Lambert-St. Louis International Airport was cloaked in a light but steady drizzle. Outside the small jet, a conservative gray Chrysler idled alongside the chain link fence that bordered the tarmac of the private landing area. The car's windshield wipers arced back and forth.

When Madison emerged from the plane, toting his single cloth suitcase, the Chrysler's lights flashed on. He approached the car and got in the front seat on the passenger side.

A black man, in his early sixties, sat waiting behind the

steering wheel. The man was solidly built, wearing a tailored coat and scarf against the evening chill, and a wide-brimmed pearl gray fedora. He had about him a quiet, stern sense of dignity. He appraised his new passenger with no show of enthusiasm.

"Madison?"

"That's right. You're Johnny's father?"

"Taylor Willow." The voice was husky, authoritative, matching his appearance. They shook hands. "I don't know exactly what Arn Shapiro expects you to accomplish, but we might as well get rolling."

The Chrysler eased away from there.

They drove in silence for a while. Mr. Willow followed the airport perimeter, then they drove west until they connected with 270 South, skirting the western border of St. Louis. In the passing lights, Madison saw that the man's face was a grim mask. The only sound in the car was the monotonous drone of the windshield wipers and the hiss of tires on wet pavement as they traveled through the night.

"Thanks for driving out to pick me up," he offered. "By way of breaking the ice, Mr. Willow, I just want you to know that I have a collection of your old gospel songs on CD."

"Thank you, son." His speaking voice had the smooth richness of warmed honey. "That was a long time ago."

"Your version of *I Surrender All* is the best version I've ever heard."

Taylor Willow continued staring straight ahead as he drove.

"Well that's music to these old ears. But, son, this here is business. I reckon Arn told you that I'm dead against him sending someone in on this. Nothing personal. But I'm not only Johnny's father, I'm also his manager. Keeping things together is *my* job. This here is a private matter, and I resent you boys sticking your noses into something that's none of your business. We can take care of our own."

"Arn told me that you and he already tangled over that. He's got an exclusive booking and promotional contract with your son, and clause nine gives Arn the right to protect his interests."

"And how do you intend to do that? He told me you're real good when it comes to angling delicate situations. You'd damn well better be if you intend to work with me on this one."

"I've been briefed, and Arn gave me a full background package," said Madison. "Tell me about this drummer who's causing all the grief."

Willow grimaced as if he'd tasted something unpleasant.

"Calls himself Eddie Chase. Shoot, we never heard of the guy before but he answered an ad in the local paper when Johnny was putting his road band together. The cat's a good drummer, so Johnny hired him. But he turned out to be a punk. Trouble. Down in Jamaica, in Kingston, while the band was having their rehearsal sessions, I found out Eddie Chase made contact with some rastas to smuggle cocaine back into the states when the band flew back after rehearsing to start this tour. Even with airport security and such, a band with tons of gear has it fairly easy with Customs, especially someone who's as well loved in the public eye as Johnny. Eddie Chase was planning to stash the stuff inside his drum kit and get it to St. Louis that way. I found out because I heard him talking on his cell phone when he didn't know I was walking by. I couldn't help but overhear and down there, they weren't even talking in code. It sounded to me like Eddie was trying to set up a long term thing."

"Did you confront him?"

"I figured Johnny should know first, to keep everything straight what with Johnny's rehab and his comeback and all. And you know what? I got the shock of my life. Johnny told me to my face that he knew all about it. He blew up at me for sticking my nose in. Said it had nothing to do with the concert or the tour and so it was none of my concern." Willow paused, then expelled a sigh. "Johnny's a good man, but he's got a hair trigger on that temper of his that can be touched off just too damn fast. But even after he cooled down some, he wouldn't tell me a thing more about it."

"So he knew what Chase was up to?"

Taylor Willow nodded. "And he didn't seem to like it none. But it was like he was resigned to it and that was that. He told me not to bring it up again and I haven't. But, well, I called Shapiro when I ran out of ideas. So I guess I've got no right to be hostile to you."

"What about Johnny's involvement in smuggling coke with Eddie Chase, despite his claiming to you and Arn and the world that he's clean? You must have thought about that since you had that talk with Johnny in Jamaica."

Willow hesitated, passing on the right side a slow-moving truck hogging the left-hand lane.

"I want you to know, I'm not just being a father. But if my son was doing hard drugs again, I'd know it."

"Maybe he's not doing them. Maybe he's just smuggling them. That's bad enough."

They had left 270 and caught I-44 East. Madison kept his eyes on the passing exit signs to pinpoint his location. They caught another exit, into the western St. Louis suburb of Webster Groves. The rain had tapered off. The Chrysler traveled sedately through a neighborhood of winding streets and upper middle class homes set back from the streets on spacious lots, separated from each other by trees and foliage.

"I got the feeling Eddie Chase is holding something over my son's head," said Taylor Willow. "He's using something to keep my Johnny in line and make him look the other way from whatever's going down."

"I'll lean on the drummer," said Madison. "But I've got a question for you. Why did you wait until this morning to call Shapiro about all of this?"

"Because things have been happening since we got back from Jamaica. But you look here, son, long as we're shooting straight with each other. I've got to get one thing perfectly clear between you and me."

"What would that be?"

"Well, Arn told me some about you and your, uh, specialties, Mr. Madison, but just the same I want to emphasize that this has to be handled as discreetly as possible if a man, well, if a man like you is going to get involved. If anything about this leaks out, Johnny's career will be stalled out for good and everything we've worked for, the cure and all of it, will have gone right down the tubes. People don't buy CD's from an artist that's hooked on hard drugs. Some of your white rock-and-roll boys have found that out the hard way, and the same with rap and R&B. Johnny's clean. But if the media ever got wind of any of this smuggling noise, well, they'd crucify us on the spot because that's the way they are." Willow struck the steering wheel angrily with a balled fist. "Johnny staging his big comeback concert right here in his hometown, and now this. It couldn't have happened at a worse time."

Madison let Willow watch the road. He was watching Willow in the passing streetlights, gauging the man's responses and body language, though Johnny's father was obviously plainspoken enough. Madison tried always to avoid family complications when working because they always resulted in muddied water, but here it couldn't be avoided.

"I've got Shapiro's take," he said. "Why don't you bring me up to speed?"

Mr. Willow's posture relaxed as he drove, indicating gratitude at having been asked.

"It got worse down in Jamaica. Tension started to build. The other members of the road band didn't know what was going on between Johnny and Eddie, whatever it was, but I saw that they could feel that something was wrong, you know? Some of the practice sessions went real bad. Musicians are good at picking up on vibes. Lana and me, we tried to talk to Johnny about it a couple of times when we were alone with him. But that son of mine can build an invisible brick wall around himself when he sets his mind to it, and he has.

"None of this has been good for Johnny. He's steaming inside and I just know that my boy's going to explode any second now. I know Johnny well enough to know that in these old bones. That temper of his will blow and he's liable to do something without warning and it could be something real stupid and that could be real bad. I know that much from experience.

"So I called Shapiro. Reckon I want to defuse a situation that hasn't happened yet."

"When did you get in from Jamaica?"

"Last night, late."

"Do you think the drummer still has this coke he brought in, if he brought it in? He sounds like a mule who's supposed to pass it straight to whoever financed him on this end."

Willow sighed again. "There's too much that I don't know. So there, you've been brought up to speed. You're here to get some answers. And you can start right now. This is where we live."

He eased the Chrysler into a sloping, paved driveway and braked to a stop.

Another car happened to be approaching from the opposite direction, and turned in behind them. Both cars doused their lights and engines.

Madison and Mr. Willow left the Chrysler. They stood before a modern, sprawling two-story home that could have been transplanted from Beverly Hills.

The car behind them was a late model Toyota Corolla. A woman alighted from the driver's side, wearing tan slacks and jacket and a black silk blouse. Madison estimated her age at nearing thirty, maybe. Her red hair was worn shoulder-length. A shoulder bag swung at her side. She had a nice figure and a wide smile.

"Taylor, welcome home from Jamaica."

They exchanged the briefest hug.

"Wish I could say it was good to be back. Hello, Carin. When did you get in?"

"This afternoon. You didn't think I'd miss Johnny's big opening show for the tour?" She glanced skyward. The drizzle had ceased, but a dampness in the air promised more to come. "I do wish Johnny was giving this concert out on the coast. It was seventy-five degrees and sunny when I left."

Her eyes shifted to Madison.

"Carin, this is Steve Madison. He represents Arn Shapiro. Steve, this is Carin Aucott. She's CEO at RockTime, the label that's releasing Johnny's new CD."

Madison had already recognized her from her pictures in the media. She had fought her way to the top of a male-controlled business, playing by no one's rules and with no one's smarts but her own.

They shook hands. Her touch was cool, as were her green eyes.

"Nice to meet you, Steve, I'm sure." Her freshness became tart. "Unfortunately, I've heard about you and the services you provide." She looked at Taylor. "What's wrong?"

Willow cleared his throat.

"Uh, I'm afraid things are a little stressed around here at the moment, Carin. There's been some trouble."

She started to reply.

The front door of the house flew open and a woman rushed out to meet them.

She was slim, in her early to mid twenties, her hair worn in a moderate length natural style. Golden loop earrings accentuated the chocolate hue of her skin, as did a light colored sheath that caressed her shapely figure as she hurried across the lawn to meet them.

In the indirect lighting from the house, she reminded Madison of something illusive; something timeless and exotic. He recognized her too, from Shapiro's background packet. She was Lana Willow, Johnny's wife.

Her expression was etched with worry lines, like marred ebony.

"Taylor, it's Johnny. He's gone. And he took his gun with him."

CHAPTER THREE

Taylor Willow touched his daughter-in-law's wrists with both of his hands.

"How long has he been gone? What happened?"

"It's my fault. I should have stayed with him like you told me to. I know how uptight he's been since we got back from Jamaica. But tonight, after you left, he seemed to calm down. Taylor, I thought he was okay."

"When did he leave?"

"No more than twenty minutes ago. I was in the shower. When I came out, he was gone. The pistol he keeps in the dresser is gone, too. Oh Taylor, I'm so sorry."

He gave her wrists a reassuring squeeze before releasing them.

"Relax, honey. That son of mine has him a mind of his own, and no mistake. No one could have stopped him if Johnny wanted to go, you know that."

Madison interjected, "Your husband gets around pretty well for a blind man."

Lana seemed to register his presence for the first time. Her eyes narrowed cautiously.

"Who are you?"

Willow introduced Madison. Lana nodded, but offered no handshake.

Taylor turned to Madison. "Damn, I should have seen this coming. I'll bet he went off to meet Eddie Chase."

"About his getting around."

"Mr. Madison, my son is a remarkable person. He even

keeps a bicycle in the garage that he pedals around on the streets out here, just for relaxation, and he's never fallen off the thing. Tonight he must have called a cab, and had it waiting for his first chance at a breakaway. It came when Lana took her shower."

"Something was said about him taking a gun."

Lana Willow said, "I have a permit and handgun training. The gun is in the house for our personal protection. But Johnny knows every inch of our house as well as a seeing man could. We kept the gun in a drawer of my bedside table."

Madison tugged at an earlobe. "So there's a blind man out on the town tonight with an attitude and a gun." He turned to Taylor. "It sure sounds like a falling out among thieves."

Lana gasped.

Willow drew his spine straight, and his expression tightened.

"I told you, Madison, this is Eddie Chase's deal. For godssakes, my son knows how much he stands to lose. Eddie is bringing in junk for somebody else and he's blackmailing Johnny into letting him get away with it. But I knew he'd push Johnny too far."

Carin Aucott kept shifting her gaze among the three of them.

"I think someone should explain to me what's going on?"

Willow started to reply.

Madison cut him off. "Save that for a minute. Where does Eddie live? And I'll need to borrow someone's car."

"You can use mine," said Carin, "if this is as urgent as it sounds."

Madison nodded his thanks and strode to the Corolla,

positioning himself behind the steering wheel.

Taylor Willow followed him. "Take I-44 into the city and get off on Tower Grove going south. Eddie's got a place on Cleveland, about a block from the Botanical Gardens." He rattled off an address that Madison memorized. "Play this any way you have to, Steve," he added. "But please keep it low key for Johnny's sake, okay?"

Madison turned the ignition key and fired up the engine.

"That's why I'm here. I'll do what needs to be done."

Lana Willow came over, and Johnny's father stepped aside in deference to her. Uncertain emotion flickered in her eyes.

"Please." Her voice pulsated with everything that was in her eyes. "Take me with you."

No man could see her now and not be touched inside. She was vulnerable, scared. But he sensed a true strength in her, too.

"I'm sorry, Lana. I've got to do this alone. You'd only be in my way."

"No, *stop*. Johnny needs me!"

"I'll bring him home, I promise." Madison looked past her at Taylor. "One thing. Will Johnny be able to line up a new drummer in time for tomorrow night's concert if he has to?"

Willow scrutinized Madison with uncertainty.

"St. Louis is a musicians' town. Yes, I imagine he could, if he had to."

Madison slipped the car into reverse.

"That's all I need to know. Keep the home fires burning."

He backed the Corolla out of the driveway and was on his way, back to the freeway and east into St. Louis, following Taylor's directions.

It was a twenty-minute drive, and his mind was busy all the way.

His sympathies were all with Johnny Willow, and not just because he was being paid to straighten up the guy's life. If Taylor Willow's reading of the situation was accurate, Johnny had given Eddie Chase a job in his band, and for thanks, the drummer had walked all over Johnny, jeopardizing Johnny's whole career. Madison wondered what Eddie Chase held over Johnny's head, again assuming that Taylor Willow's reading could be taken at face value. Thus far, Madison had little else to go on. There was the possibility that Taylor was wrong, that Johnny was backsliding from his cure and was a willing partner with Chase in a drug smuggling operation.

And if Johnny was *not* at Eddie's?

In that case, Madison intended to lean on Eddie Chase and hard. He would get to the bottom of and nullify whatever it was that Chase had on Johnny. If it was physical evidence of some sort, he would retrieve it. If it was something else, he would convince the drummer that it would be prudent to stay the hell out of Johnny Willow's life.

The address on Cleveland belonged to a shabby little house of the box-like frame style that went up by the millions in America after World War II. Outward suburban expansion had left this residential neighborhood behind decades ago.

He parked the Corolla at the curb, two look-alike houses down, and walked back. The evening chill was damp and penetrating. Despite this, he wore his jacket open. He wanted his shoulder-holstered .44 to be within easy reach.

At the front door of Eddie Chase's house, he stood to one side and delivered a brisk double knock.

A moment of silence, then footsteps.

The door opened.

He was surprised to find a young white woman standing there. She was a petite blonde, hardly more than seventeen or eighteen years old. A cute upturned nose was sprinkled with girlish freckles. But Madison's overall first impression was one of dissipation. He had seen her kind often enough in his work for Arn and during his own musician days. Concert rats. Groupies. Runaways, most of them. This little blonde in a breast-peaked white T-shirt and jeans wore the washed-out signs of addiction—sunken eyes despite her youth and beauty, unnaturally pale complexion—and there was about her that taint of defeat and resignation that came to all of them sooner rather than later, unless they grew up and wised up and got out before it was too late.

Her eyes were wary. Her hand stayed on the doorknob.

"Yes?"

"Is Eddie home?"

"Who wants to know?"

Madison brought up a foot to waist level and kicked the door inward. She stumbled back with a shout. The door swung in but met resistance before it could meet the wall. There came a startled grunt, male variety. Madison entered the house, kicking the door shut behind him. He was in a small living room appointed with thrift store furnishings.

A black man had been waiting behind the door, his back pressed to the wall. He now went into a low crouch like an animal ready to attack. The guy looked like a drummer; thin, bantam sized, with the wired eyes of a cokehead. His head was shaved. He wore a white two-strap undershirt, baggy black denims, high top sneakers, with an oversized medallion hanging from a heavy gold chain around his scrawny neck. He held a pistol.

43

Madison sidestepped and caught the man's gun wrist with both hands even as the gun was tracking up in his direction, then in one continuous movement he executed a flip and Eddie Chase was fulcrummed over his back and sailed head-over-heels across the room to smash, upside down, into a wall with such force that the whole house seemed to shudder.

The gun flew from Eddie's fingers. He collapsed ungracefully into a heap on the floor and tried to get up. Madison moved in again and kicked hard with his right shoe, connecting with Eddie's jaw, tossing him onto his back. Eddie lay there, rubbing his jaw, looking up at the ceiling, stunned and groaning.

Madison leaned over and picked up the gun, a Colt .38 Detective Special.

"Okay, kids. Let's play Q and A."

The blonde ran over to Eddie and knelt down beside him.

"Eddie! Eddie, are you all right?"

Chase managed to sit up. He thrust her away from him.

"Get the hell off me, bitch." He stood shakily, his coked-up eyes glaring at Madison. "Who are *you,* man?"

"I represent people who have an interest in Johnny Willow," said Madison. "What happened between you and Johnny in Kingston?"

"I don't know what you're talking about."

Madison gestured with the .38.

"Who were you waiting for, with this, when I showed up instead? Did someone tell you that Johnny's running around loose tonight with a gun?"

The blonde's eyes were wide with her coke high and with fear.

"Eddie, jeez, tell him what he wants to know. He's got a gun!"

Chase ignored her.

44

"I got tired of being under the gun." He flung the words at Madison in a torrent of emotion. "I decided to give someone else a chance to see what it feels like."

There was a knock at the door.

The blonde girl made a terrified sound.

Eddie shifted his attention to the door with a tightening of his body.

Madison said, "Now who could that be?"

Chase gulped audibly. Beads of perspiration were like pearls along his hairline.

"Look, dog, why don't we just cut? I don't want trouble for Johnny. I don't want trouble from him, either. I don't want trouble with nobody. You tell that to Johnny and his daddy. I'll quit the band, that's cool. But right now—"

Another knock, harder this time. Insistent.

"Tell Johnny for yourself," said Madison. "Open the door, Eddie."

"You don't understand, man—"

Madison gestured with the .38.

"I said open the door, Eddie."

Eddie looked from Madison to the blonde, then back at Madison, especially at the gun. He rose to his feet and crossed to the front door. He took a deep breath, and opened it.

Johnny Willow stood on the doorstep. Madison saw a taxicab pulling away from the curb out front. Johnny wore a cream single-breasted tuxedo jacket over a velour tracksuit, black velour slacks and white Flashback sneakers. His wrap-around sunglasses reflected the room lights as white pin-points.

Madison recognized him from Johnny's CD's and videos. Johnny had finely chiseled facial features and the slight awkwardness and wraparound shades of the blind.

But he stood there with a poise that was its own pride, a younger version of the quiet dignity of his father.

Eddie pasted on a nervous smile.

"Well hey, Johnny. What up, dog? I, uh, wasn't expecting you."

Johnny stepped in with his arm up and out, and stiff-armed Eddie back into the house. Eddie stumbled. Johnny followed him in. He appeared to be working hard at self-control. He bristled with anger.

"I know you wasn't expecting me, pimp. That's why I'm here. You and me got a score to settle."

Before Eddie could reply, Madison spoke up from across the room.

"Come on in, Johnny. But stay cool."

If Johnny was surprised to hear another voice, which he must have been, he didn't let it show. His shaded eyes snapped in Madison's direction. His hand slid into a pocket of the velour jacket.

"Who am I talking to?"

"Your father sent me."

Johnny's hand stayed in his pocket.

"Like hell."

"I'm holding a gun," said Madison. "Take your hand out of your pocket and leave your gun where it is."

Eddie Chase placed himself behind Madison. He snickered.

"A blind guy come to shoot the place up? That's funny."

"Shut up," said Madison. His attention remained on the man in the doorway. "Johnny, my name is Steve Madison. There's no need for violence. Let's you and me and Eddie sit down and talk and see what we can come up with."

Johnny started to say something.

Before he could, three oversized men stormed him from

46

behind, forcing Johnny into the house and slamming the door shut after them.

These intruders were Caucasian bruisers of linebacker proportions, togged casually in windbreakers and the like. Each man held a pistol. Whoever they were, they behaved like professionals.

One of them, with a .45 automatic, spoke up, his eyes having acknowledged Eddie Chase, Johnny, and the girl as if he'd expected them to be here. His flinty eyes and the .45's muzzle centered on Madison.

"Heard what you just said about coming up with something. Why don't we start with you? Drop the piece and show us some pedigree." He raised the .45 automatic until the muzzle was pointed at the bridge of Madison's nose. "And make it good, dude, or you're dead."

CHAPTER FOUR

Madison released Eddie's .38. It dropped to the threadbare carpet. He still had the .44 in his shoulder rig, but a lot of good that did him now.

For an instant, the tableau held in Eddie Chase's living room, allowing Madison a rapid survey of the factions confronting each other.

Johnny Willow was visibly seething with anger, but for the moment was holding it in check.

Eddie Chase and his woman child, the weak intimidated by the strong; the blonde stood at his side, and they seemed to be quaking with wide-eyed fear, drawing back from the three gunmen who had forced their way in.

And the men themselves. Where did they fit in? Two of them had positioned themselves to either side of the front door.

The tableau unfroze.

Johnny Willow growled deep in his throat and his right hand darted for his jacket pocket.

The man who had been facing Madison swung his .45 around with dazzling speed and rammed the muzzle into Johnny's throat, tilting the blind man's head back.

"Don't even think about it, boy. You being a super star don't mean squat to me. Let's see your hand out empty or I'll blow your brains out."

"He'll do it, Johnny," said Madison. "Don't be stupid."

Johnny's hand came out, empty.

The bruiser approached him and reached into Johnny's

jacket pocket. He withdrew a .38 pistol like Eddie's, only with a longer barrel.

"Damn. Blind boys can get hurt playing with guns." He hefted the gun absently and dropped it into his pocket. Then he turned to Eddie Chase. "You know why we're here."

Eddie looked like he wanted to become invisible.

"Yeah, yeah, I know."

"We come for the stuff and we find a goddamn party in progress." He looked back at Madison and returned the .45's muzzle to again being aimed directly between Madison's eyes. "Now let's see some I.D., dude. I've still got to decide what to do with you."

The only door out of the living room, other than the front door, was to Eddie's left. The instant the man's attention had turned to Madison, Eddie dashed through that doorway.

The man maintained the .45's bead on Madison.

"Danny, Len. Get that little punk." He barked like a field marshal. "He gets away and Pete will have our heads."

They took off running.

The sound of a car starting came from behind the house, then explosions of gunfire, magnified by the stillness of the night, almost drowning out the shifting of gears, the squealing of tires. There came the pounding of shoe leather, and Danny and Len ran back in.

"The little weasel got away, Carlo," said Len.

"Those shots will bring down the cops." Carlo indicated Johnny. "Okay, we take the nigger. That will have to do for now." He glared at the blonde. "You. Get lost and forget this ever happened. Do you understand me?"

She cringed in a corner, reminding Madison of a frightened child.

"Yes, sir."

"That's good. I ever see you again, I'll twist off your head and stuff it up your you-know-what."

The girl appeared to shrink into the corner, wide-eyed, nodding and nodding frantically.

Madison charged in low at Carlo while the man was addressing the girl and they both went lurching to the floor, landing full force on their sides, struggling with each other. Carlo raised the .45. Madison tilted his head and raised his left shoulder slightly as they grappled. Carlo commenced clubbing him viciously with the gun butt, and Madison reacted with a snort of pain as if he really felt it. He fought a little more, for effect, then collapsed to lie, groaning, with his nose buried in the carpet.

Carlo got to his feet. Madison sensed him pulling a foot back for a kick, but there wasn't a thing Madison could do about it without giving away the fact that he was feigning unconsciousness. The kick caught him in the right side and hurt as much as he expected. He rode with it, forcing himself not to groan with the pain that exploded through him.

Then Carlo addressed his crew.

"All right, let's get the boy out of here. *Move!*"

"Boy, hell!" Johnny's snarl was ferocious.

There was a flurry of earnest movement, a struggle, then an expulsion of breath and the clout of a blunt instrument, a gun butt, striking bone. The exhalation of breath, sounds of a body sagging, being caught, and an unconscious man's feet being dragged across the carpet and out through the front door. These sounds came magnified to Madison's ear at floor level.

Carlo was saying to the blonde, "Stay until you hear us gone, then you're on your own. And you remember what I told you."

He slapped her. Madison heard the blow slam her into

the wall. Then Carlo was gone. The front door slammed.

Madison leapt to his feet and threw a glance at the girl.

She was crouched on the floor in the corner, crying delicately to herself. There was the red welt of a hand mark across one side of her face. She looked in a state of shock and appeared years younger, like a child.

"I don't understand." Tears ran down her cheeks. "Where did Eddie go? He knows I love him. He promised that he'd always take me with him. Where did he go?"

Madison was already heading for the door.

"He just showed you what kind of a guy he is. Now go home to wherever that is and finish growing up, and be thankful for life's little lessons. You're getting off easy, kid."

Then he was out the door and hustling down the sidewalk toward Carin Aucott's Corolla.

Twin tail lights, which could only belong to the vehicle carrying Johnny Willow given the less than sixty seconds since they'd dragged him out of the house, were rounding a corner at the far end of the block.

Sirens were approaching from not far away, from more than one direction.

He jumped behind the Corolla's steering wheel and goosed the engine to life. Headlights off, he rounded the corner at the far end of the block about thirty seconds behind the first car.

The darkened glass dome of the botanical gardens that Taylor Willow had mentioned passed by on Madison's left as he followed the tail lights north on a street called Tower Grove, pacing himself about a quarter mile behind the first vehicle in the sparse nighttime traffic. Eventually he had to run the risk of turning on his headlights.

From this distance, the lead car looked like a Cadillac. It

led Madison in a northwesterly course away from where Eddie Chase lived, first connecting with I-44 West, then cutting north across town on a street called Hampton until they hit the Daniel Boone Expressway, again tracking west. Traffic was heavier on the expressway even at this late hour on a Thursday night, but Madison was able to keep the lead car—it was a Cadillac—in clear view.

What the hell was happening? he wondered as he drove. What had he stumbled into? His job tonight should have been cut and dry. Should have been. Neutralize Eddie Chase as any sort of threat to Johnny, and keep the cork on things. Elementary, for a Shapiro job. Except that Eddie Chase was presently among the missing, and three guys— three mobster-type guys—had Johnny and were taking him to see someone named Pete.

Yeah. Elementary as hell.

Forty minutes after leaving Eddie Chase's, the Cadillac exited the expressway, soon finding the sedate streets of a suburb that the off-ramp sign had identified as Ladue. Another money neighborhood. Big money. Homes were set far back from the road. The ones Madison saw were palatial. Some of the properties were walled in from view of the road.

He cut his headlights and continued to follow the tail lights that wended through the back roads of the suburb. Traffic was practically nonexistent.

Another mile and a half and the lead car's brake lights flashed. It turned into one of the walled properties and disappeared from sight.

CHAPTER FIVE

Madison killed his engine and glided the Corolla to a soundless stop at the base of the high brick wall surrounding the property.

There was a vapor lamp over the main gate some one hundred yards further along the wall, but that illumination did not reach to this point, where the towering brick wall managed to create deeper shadows within the gloom.

A breeze rustled tree branches. The rain still had not resumed but the sky remained close, starless.

The breeze carried the sound of indiscernible voices, then a house door being closed.

Then, nothing.

He reached overhead and unscrewed the covering and bulb of the car's dome light. He opened the car door and alighted as quietly as possible. He felt as one with the night, and hurried to one of several towering oak trees that fronted the wall on the outside. He gained the top of the wall with little effort and pressed himself against it to get his bearings.

From atop the wall, he could see that the grounds of the estate sloped upward toward the main house. Lights shone from the ground floor of a house that was similar to the spreads he'd observed on the drive here. A four-car garage was dark, as were the vague shapes of outbuildings of various types. He saw a pinpoint red glow of a cigarette being smoked to the left of the front door of the house.

There was a guardhouse just inside the front gate, but

Madison could see no one there. Then a man's coarse laugh drifted to him on the breeze.

He pressed himself to the cold brick of the wall top.

Three men were advancing along the inside of the wall, conversing among themselves. Two of them toted shoulder-slung automatic weapons. There was some grumbling, and Madison found himself cracking a smile at the briefest memory of his own sentry duty-pulling days in the military. The night shift was never fun on a damp, cold night like this. He realized that he was holding his breath. The sentries passed beneath his position, not looking up.

He watched them reach the guardhouse. Then he dropped from the top of the wall to land with a complete absence of sound on the grassy turf inside the base of the wall. He broke from the wall, jogging in a low crouch across the gloomy expanse of lawn to the southern wall of the main house, gaining a point beyond view of those by the sentry shed. He grabbed the wall with his back and drew the .44, holding it up and ready in a two-handed grip.

The man he'd seen minutes earlier, posted at the front door, smoking, chose that moment to walk around to this side of the house, probably to take a leak. It was Len.

He emitted a startled grunt but no more when Madison swung hard with the side of his hand and caught him behind the left ear with a sharp blow from the butt of the .44. Len's knees buckled and he fell to the ground and commenced snoring gently. Madison made quick work of concealing Len as best he could behind shrubbery in the deepest shadows at the base of the house.

There was a back door in the center of this side of the house. Madison approached and eased the door handle open, stepping into a corridor.

He knelt there, his senses probing this alien, hostile environment. This part of the interior of the house was shrouded in a hushed semi-gloom. He could see that this corridor sported cabinets to either side, ending in a kitchen, and there was light beyond.

No one was in sight.

But he heard voices.

He followed them, stepping through the kitchen, moving like a cat across a plushly carpeted, well-appointed living room with a vaulted ceiling, drawn curtains, and subtle illumination from a single corner lamp.

The voices became clearer.

He hugged the wall of a carpeted hallway that fed onto the living room and paused beside an open doorway. The corridor was dim, illuminated only by the light from the living room and the triangle of light that spilled from this doorway.

Madison paused, and listened.

Johnny sat there on the couch, listening to the men he could not see; listening to them talk, and listening to them move. He could *see* them in his mind's eye, his every sense other than sight having been honed by a lifetime spent in blindness.

They reeked of male cologne. They would be well heeled, no doubt. His surroundings had that Benjamin vibe. Big money.

He was in the world of that TV show, *The Sopranos*, and *The Godfather*. He watched movies and TV just like he could now see what was going on around him. He had little difficulty navigating in a seeing person's world. Hell, he was packing heat, or had been until that cab dropped him at Eddie Chase's and this crazy ride began.

Sure, he knew where he was and who these people were.

He'd already declined the offer of a drink. He sat with his back straight and his head held high, as if unaware or indifferent to the fact that a trio of armed men had brought him here.

No one had spoken a word during the drive here from Eddie Chase's, and he'd been satisfied to ride in silence. He'd passed the trip taking himself out of that moment.

In the day, smack had done it for him just as it had for those geniuses who'd been his heroes coming up, guys like Miles and all the be-bop jazz guys. Heroin provided a cocoon from the hurt and anxieties of reality, and if there was a better high, God had kept it for Himself. But he'd fought back from the ultimately debilitating addiction that had almost destroyed his life, his career and his marriage. With the help of Lana and his father and God, through prayer and tricks he'd picked up from his audio books on Eastern religions, he'd found his way back to sanity, back to the real world, within the walls of that rehab center, that ability to "cocoon" himself without drugs whenever he wanted or needed to.

Wrapped in his own silence, sitting in the backseat of the car between two of his abductors while the third drove, he'd let his mind trace back to when he was twelve years old, in the choir in his father's church where Johnny Willow first sang from his heart and brought other people to their feet. *Wade in the Water* had been Johnny's favorite. Still was, for that matter, and on this night he had truly experienced again, if only within his mind and body, the *heat* of those services in that funky old ghetto Baptist church. He heard again the hallelujahs, the stomping and the tambourines. Sweet soul music, yes, and his supple young voice glided again over the playing of the fervent church band for enthusiastic call and response with the parishioners while the full-bodied baritone of his father needed no microphone to exhort his congregation. Yes, it was real, and he lived it again in his mind.

But that was gone now.

He knew what was going on *here* in this big house where they'd brought him. What he didn't know was who was the cat who'd been at Eddie Chase's? Madison, he called himself. Steve Madison. That was the head-messer. Who was Steve Madison, and where was he now?

"You know what I want," the man in charge here was saying. The rustle of the material of his clothing said he was dressed differently from the others. Johnny detected the rustle of silk, and the scent of talc. "I know you're a public person. This here's an important time in your career, or so I'm told. We want to keep this quiet too."

"I bet you do."

"Now don't get mouthy with me, boy. I'm trying to be hospitable here."

"Sure, you are. That's why three guys with guns brought me here under force. Three guys for one blind man. You jokers must be real tough."

"Okay, screw it." The voice grew tight and mean. "Tell me where Eddie Chase took off to with my shipment of coke."

"I don't know what you're talking about. I don't know anything about any coke."

A rustle of material, and Johnny knew that the speaker moved to stand before him, no doubt intimidating to a man who could see.

"I am not fooling around, boy. I had contacts down in Kingston watching every move you and your bunch made while you were down there. See, I like to protect my investments. Me and Eddie, we had us a deal."

"That was you and Eddie." Inside, Johnny expected to be physically struck at any moment but he tried not to let that show. "What's any of this got to do with me?"

"Do you know who I am?"

What the hell, thought Johnny.

"My guess is that you're Pete Santini." Johnny lifted his face as a seeing man would if admiring his surroundings. "That must put me in a right nice part of town."

"I know your father talked to you about it in Jamaica," said Santini, "and you didn't do a thing to interfere. You told your old man to butt out."

"How do you know these things?"

"I told you. Contacts. I'd say you let Eddie come back into the States with my shipment hid inside his equipment, like Eddie told me he planned, because he was giving you a piece of the action. Maybe in cash, maybe in coke. So now I'm only going to ask one more time, superstar. Where's Eddie? He expected my boys to show up, then you and some other guy horned in and now the little weasel has disappeared. And I want him. He's still got my shipment. He started putting my people off after he got back from Jamaica because he said the band's equipment was being delayed in transit. That didn't sound so good, and tonight I told him the deal was down and I sent Carlo and the boys. They weren't after you. But he got away because of you. Why did you show up at his place tonight?"

"It was about something else. I don't know where he is."

"And that's all you've got to say?"

"It's all I know, *boy.*"

"Carlo," said Santini. "Go out to that shelf in the garage and bring back the pliers. I think we're going to have to pull some teeth."

"Right, Mr. Santini."

Madison chose that moment to make his entrance, the Magnum held at his side.

"Hold on, Carlo. You're not going anywhere."

It was a man's study, all deep carpeting, walls lined with leather bound books and framed prints, and polished heavy wood-and-leather furniture.

The man called Santini stood in front of the desk, towering over Johnny, though the blind man did not appear to be intimidated. Santini was in his mid-thirties. Handsome, dark, with classic Mediterranean features. He wore a belted, burgundy smoking jacket, woven with a gold design, over pale blue pajamas. His slippers were Gucci.

Danny, the other half of Carlo's crew, stood behind Johnny.

Carlo was halfway to the door, and froze with a startled expression on his burly features when he saw Madison. Then he made a blurred motion with his right hand, reaching for a concealed weapon.

"Don't." Madison did not raise the Magnum from his side, but something in his voice checked Carlo's reflex. "I know I'm trespassing. I don't like trespassers. I don't want trouble." He looked at Santini. "I've come for Johnny."

Santini chuckled, and stroked his chin, regarding Madison as if with genuine amusement.

"I see. So put away the piece, why don't you? How long have you been listening? We're just having us a friendly conversation here."

"That's why no one's dead," said Madison, "yet. Come on, Johnny."

Santini faced Madison head-on.

"Hold up, here. You are trespassing, bub. And breaking and entering. How did you get past my boys outside?"

Madison knew a diversionary tactic when he heard it,

and his peripheral vision caught Danny speed-drawing a .357 from under his jacket, already tracking the pistol at Madison in target acquisition. Madison raised the Magnum and squeezed off a shot that hammered the eardrums within the confines of the study.

The round took Danny high in the chest and kicked him over like a hammer blow to the floor. Danny did not move. There was lots of blood.

Gunsmoke hazed lazily in the air.

Santini glanced from the corpse on the floor up to Madison. He didn't look overly alarmed. But he had stopped stroking his chin.

"I think we can forget about trespassing. That was murder."

"That was self-defense. I forget, Santini. Is kidnapping a capital offense in this state?" Madison looked at the man seated on the couch. "You were brought here under duress, right, Johnny?"

Johnny rose to his feet. Johnny winced at the powerful blast, but otherwise retained a stoic demeanor.

"It was kidnapping and nothing but."

"Well there you are," said Madison to Santini. "We're leaving . . . after I settle a debt."

He swung the Magnum with all his might, and the pistol grip snapped into Carlo's temple.

Carlo collapsed into an ungainly, unconscious pile on the floor near the corpse.

Johnny grinned at the sounds. "Damn, I like the way you handle yourself, brother."

Santini snickered. "You know you're a dead man, right?" he asked Madison. "You'll never make it off this property alive."

Madison sniffed. "I smell Mafia. Don't you boys have

60

your own drug pipelines set up for bringing in cocaine? What's this all about?"

The rumble of running, trampling feet could be heard advancing in a hurry down the hallway beyond the study door.

Santini's lips curled.

"Now what, wise guy?"

Madison moved, double-time, behind Santini, his left arm wrapping across the man's throat. He jerked the head back violently and, at the same time, he rammed two inches of the Magnum's barrel up Santini's rear end, pajamas and all.

"Now we walk out of here." Madison held the guy flush against him, and was practically whispering in his ear. "And if one of your soldiers even looks like he wants to rock and roll, Petey, guess who gets it first where it hurts the most?" He gave the gun an extra, ungentle nudge for emphasis. "Get me?"

The doorway became filled with the men Madison had evaded outside. The ones behind held rifles, the one in front, a pistol.

"Mr. Santini, we heard—"

The point man stopped, his mind trying to register what his eyes were seeing. The sentries behind bumped into him, slapstick-style.

Madison nudged the .44 again, rougher than before.

"Time to make an executive decision, Petey. Do Johnny and I walk out, or do you kiss life goodbye the hard way?"

Santini didn't miss a beat.

"Cool, boys." His voice was as calm as someone asking for a glass of water.

A heartbeat while everyone held his breath. But in this world, the word of Pete Santini was the law.

"All right, guys." The point man spoke over his shoulder, not taking his attention off the scene confronting him as if he still couldn't believe his eyes. "Uh, you heard Mr. Santini. Everyone step aside and let them pass. Lower your guns."

"Not good enough," said Madison. "I want them way out of the way, Pete. I want them to leave their guns behind and after that I don't even want to see their ugly faces."

Santini nodded.

"Take them downstairs to the game room," he told the point man. "Wait for me down there. Let us pass. And no screwups, dammit. Do what I say. I don't want anyone getting in our way."

Johnny wore a wide grin. "Now that's more like it."

Rifles and pistols were placed upon the threshold, reluctantly but obediently, and with uncertain backward glances, the men traipsed back down the hall. The sound of their footfalls receded to nothing.

"Okay, Boss," said Madison. "Let's take a walk." And to the blind man, "Are you with me, Johnny?"

"Hell, yeah." Johnny chortled. "Partner, I am with you *all* the way."

Santini remained muted as Madison crab-walked him out of the house taking the same route by which he'd entered, never once relinquishing the grip of his left arm across Santini's throat or removing the gun barrel from its nesting place. They stepped outside, into the night.

It had started raining again while Madison had been inside: a cold, steady drizzle like before, just enough to be uncomfortable and make the sloping lawn slippery and treacherous, especially for two men traveling the way Madison and Santini were. It was slow going, but the three of them made it to the sentry shed without mishap and

62

through the wrought iron front gate, which they found open.

When they reached the Corolla, Madison released Santini and stepped back.

"Thanks for the hospitality, creep. Say hi to the birdies."

The .44 made a quick, short arc and connected with Santini's skull. Santini gave a peculiar slow sigh and folded to the ground.

"Sounds like you just settled another debt," said Johnny.

"Yeah, but it'll be their turn next if we don't cut fast. Here's the car. Watch your head."

The warning proved unnecessary. Johnny crossed around in front of the car with a self-assured economy of movement, his fingertips lightly grazing the car's body. Without hesitation, he found the door handle on the passenger side and slid in next to Madison in the vehicle.

Madison kicked the engine to life and sped away, fishtailing around in a noisy circle, kicking up a cloud of gravel and dirt, traveling with lights off.

Rosa snapped a final series of pictures with the infrared telephoto lens of the Corolla speeding away from the inert heap upon the ground that was Peter Santini.

"Now that's something you don't see every day."

They had been on stakeout since dusk, parked a quarter mile away.

Delahant lowered his infrared binoculars to the car seat. He turned the ignition key and the Buick purred to life. He pulled away with lights off.

"Do we call this in?"

"What for? Looked to me like our mystery man in the Corolla could be on our side."

Delahant activated the windshield wipers against the

drizzling rain beading upon the glass, blurring the Corolla's tail lights that were like tiny red eyes receding in the distance.

They passed the front gate to the Santini estate at an increasing rate of speed, headlights on.

Santini's security crew was pouring through the front gate en masse to solicitously swarm over that inert heap on the ground.

They had driven in silence for nearly ten minutes before Johnny expended a sigh that sounded as if it came from down around his ankles.

"You know I appreciate this, man, but, uh, you just killed a dude back there."

"If I'm any judge of hoods, Santini won't report it. He'll disappear Danny Boy. He doesn't want the heat. But it's your reaction I'm interested in. Yeah, Johnny, I just offed a man who was drawing a weapon on me. I was trained to do that. But you're not ruffled by it much, are you?"

"I'm a preacher's son," said Johnny, "but those were some damn mean streets I grew up on. Half the guys I went to high school with are dead from gunshot wounds."

Madison's eyes were on the rearview mirrors. There was a set of headlights way back, like tiny silver eyes watching from a distance. Or innocent people driving this same road. He couldn't be sure.

Johnny's face was turned toward him.

"Steve Madison, huh? I like your style, sure do. But how much do you know about what's been going down tonight?"

"I'd rather spend time talking about what I don't know. I just yanked you from a very difficult situation, Johnny. Show me some gratitude, why don't you? Talk to me."

The headlights were gaining on the Corolla. Madison

gripped the .44 Magnum in his right hand.

Johnny tensed. "We're not out of the woods yet, are we?"

A red light began flashing atop the roof of the pursuing vehicle. No siren, just the flasher. The car was right on their tail now, the driver rapidly alternating his headlights from low beam to high beam and back again, signaling the Corolla to pull over.

Madison began applying the brakes, easing the Corolla onto the gravel shoulder.

"This may be the law, maybe not. Let's find out. Be ready for anything."

Johnny grinned a tight grin. "With you, Madison, I got a feeling that's a way of life."

He braked to a complete stop, keeping the engine on idle, his foot hovering near the accelerator.

The tracking vehicle eased in behind them. The driver doused his lights and flasher. The car was a Buick with the flasher clamped to the roof above the door on the driver's side.

A man emerged from the passenger's side. He strode over, approaching the driver's side of the Corolla.

Madison slid his .44 lower beside his bucket seat, out of sight from his window. His right index finger remained curled around the trigger.

The man leaned over and his face seemed to fill the window. He thrust something forward for them to see.

It was not a gun. It was a slim leather packet containing identification.

"Drug Enforcement Administration. Step out of the car, both of you."

Johnny exhaled another sigh. "Oh, hell."

CHAPTER SIX

The DEA agents were named Rosa and Delahant.

Rosa was the older of the two, somewhere in his fifties. He had jowls, five-o'clock-shadow and bags under his eyes. He was slightly overweight.

Delahant, behind the wheel of the Buick, was crewcut, blond-haired, muscular and twenty years younger than Rosa was. There was a dangerous, competent look about him.

Both men were brusque.

Madison and Johnny sat in the backseat.

Madison had holstered his pistol in full view of Rosa, who had been the one to approach the Corolla. Rosa's hand stayed beneath the lapel of his jacket, and Madison knew that hand would be gripping a concealed pistol. And the driver of the Buick would have had Madison's head in his sights. Madison didn't stand a chance, and so he took no chances. But he thought it was a good sign, them letting him hold onto the gun. They considered him an ally and Johnny a victim, which was right enough and he hoped he read them right. These two had done hard time on the same dark side of the street he had spent so many years walking, except that their dirty war was being fought on the streets of American cities like St. Louis.

After Rosa had led them back to the unmarked car, and after Delahant showed his I.D., the interrogation began.

Rose sat sideways in the front seat, his features limned in the dashboard lights, his arm resting across the car seat as he stared at Madison.

"First thing we need to see is some of your identification."

Johnny began, "My name is—"

"I know your name. My daughter's got every Johnny Willow CD that ever came out." His cop eyes kept lasering in on Madison. "You're the mystery man. We've got some handle on what's shaking tonight. I can understand Santini wanting to have a word with Johnny, but what about you? Let's have some pedigree."

This was the second time tonight that someone had used those same words, and it occurred to Madison that even Johnny did not know his "pedigree," did not know who he was or why he had come to Johnny's assistance at such risk to himself to the extent of killing a man. Madison saw no reason to mention that, and he showed them his I.D. and explained to them, and to Johnny, why he was interested in Johnny's welfare. He also avoided mentioning Arn Shapiro by name, but the agents didn't seem to care.

He finished with, "I didn't know Big Brother was watching. Where did you guys come from?"

"Routine surveillance of Santini," said Rosa. "We know about Eddie Chase from wiretaps on Santini, and that something was going down. Someone ought to tell drug dealers not to use cell phones, and their codes are too stupid not to break. Anyway, we had a man watching Eddie Chase's place, and the thing with you and Santini's people went down so quick all he could do was get word to us."

Johnny made a discontented noise. "Thanks for coming to back us up."

Delahant spoke for the first time. "Mr. Santini is a respectable citizen."

"Sure he is," said Madison. "That's why he's under surveillance and wiretapped."

"It's why lawyers invented the word 'alleged.' We saw the car with Mr. Willow go in. We saw you go in, Madison, over the wall like a commando. What's your background, anyway?"

"Do I have to?"

Rosa chuckled. "Modest?"

"As hell. And I figure you guys are busy, and you intend to let us go when you're through with us here." He nodded to the small computer monitor setup beside the Buick's dash radio. "You'll have everything you can get on my background downloaded before Johnny and I have made it back to my car. I've given you what I can."

Delahant eyed him sharply in the rearview mirror. "You're a nervy bastard."

Madison nodded. "That's my nature. I take it Santini is the mob's big guy in town."

Rosa seemed never to blink, as if the laser beams from his heavily lidded, pouchy eyes could penetrate the mind if he tried hard enough.

"He's the one, but there was a time when that meant more than it does now. Everyone knows how the mob guys got aced out of the crack boom in the ghetto that started in the nineties, back when the street gangs set up their own pipelines to Colombia and Jamaica and Mexico. Economic tough times mean tough times for the mob too, and that's what tonight is about. Our intel is that Santini does not want to lose those concessions that are his. Is that enough information for you?" Then he looked at the man sitting next to Madison. "What did they want, Johnny?"

Johnny hesitated, and cleared his throat. "They wanted a shipment of cocaine that Eddie Chase brought in. They thought I was in on it. I imagine because of my past and you guys being narcs, that you'll think the same thing."

Rosa's expression softened a bit. "Don't worry, son. We know you're clean on this."

"Then what have you got to lose by sharing more intel with me?" said Madison. "I'm not going to be one of Santini's favorite people after the way I left him. He didn't look any older than thirty-six or so. That's awful young to be top mob man in a city like this."

Delahant's eyes never left Madison's in the interior rearview mirror.

"We had a gang war last year." It was if he were reading from a report. "Most of the old bosses were whacked by jacked-up punks off the street, the black gangs, and a West Coast Asian connection and a Jamaican posse was trying to buy in too. Santini managed to survive and has managed to establish a loose coalition with the street factions so that he gets a cut of what's coming in."

Rosa picked up the conversational ball.

"A banger they call Libra runs the ghetto franchise for Santini. Libra got his name from working the scales so heavy when he first started out wholesaling crack. But the word is that Libra's through cutting Santini a percentage just to keep the peace."

"Libra is preparing a concerted push to break out on his own with the whole damn city as his franchise," said Delahant, "running the streets from the bottom up, you might say."

Across the country, urban areas were in the grip of gang war bloodshed unlike anything experienced on the American scene since the bootleg wars of the Prohibition era. Neighborhood street gangs warred over distribution of an illegal substance, in this case primarily rock cocaine, or "crack." An industrious gang like Libra's could gross more than a million dollars per week.

Madison tugged at an earlobe.

"I get it. If Santini's taking a cut, he's tracking what comes in through the established connections. So Libra needs a pipeline that's his alone to finance this push you're talking about. And that's where Johnny comes into it. His drummer sets up the connection for Libra while the band is rehearsing in Jamaica."

Johnny frowned. "Santini told me Eddie was bringing in a shipment of coke for him."

Rosa snickered. "He was lying. Eddie was a mule for Libra. That shipment was to be used against Santini. Pete knows that. He must have thought he'd turned Eddie but the punk disappeared with the shipment, and Pete was hoping that you'd be his handle to finding Eddie since Eddie is your drummer."

"Was," said Johnny.

"Whatever," said Delahant.

"Let's stay centered," said Rosa. "Eddie ran in a load for Libra. A traveling band with a show like Johnny's can run into the tons with the lights, stage gear, everything else. That's how Eddie got it in, and he retrieved it once they were back on U.S. soil and has it stashed somewhere now."

"How much was Chase bringing in?"

"Half a kilo. It was a milk run and sample shipment for Libra to check for quality of product."

"That's still a lot of money on the street corner," said Madison. "The connection in Jamaica has already processed the stuff. Libra puts out a chump change seven grand investment and when he gets the stuff from Eddie, boom, he's in business, ready to sell five thousand chunks of crack at thirty dollars per vial. If he likes the quality, six months from now he's doing a hundred times that."

"If Santini lets him get away with it," said Delahant.

"That's why Eddie Chase and this coke shipment of his are so important."

Rosa nodded. "That shipment Eddie has is Libra's grubstake."

Delahant shifted his eyes from the mirror to study his partner with a funny expression. "Grubstake? Man, you've seen too many cowboy movies."

Rosa shifted his gaze from the back seat. "And what's wrong with the Duke? When I retire, I'm going to do nothing but watch westerns. That was a simpler time, damn it, and a better time." He glanced at Madison and chuckled. "Come to think of it, son, you were mighty wild west back there with Pete Santini. You always so high handed?"

"I do what they pay me to do," said Madison. "Do you mind me asking what angle you guys are working?"

"We're out to nail Santini," said Rosa. "You saw the neighborhood he lives in. Millionaires' row. He's having trouble with the gangs on the street but he's still running every illegal scam in this town. We can knock the mob's legs out from under them in St. Louis if we lean on Libra hard enough to get what he knows about Santini's drug involvement, which is everything. Then we'd have our case on Santini. We thought we had Libra on the murder of a rapper three months ago, but he's clean on that, or at least we couldn't trace him."

"You guys are mighty obliging to a vigilante like me, what with you being Federal agents and all."

Delahant grimaced, and his eyes reconnected with Madison's in the rearview.

"Is that a crack?"

"I just want you guys to understand one thing," said Johnny. "I had nothing to do with what went down between this Libra dude and Eddie; you know what I mean? I wasn't hip to what Eddie was up to until the equipment was already packed up, with the shipment in it, the day before we split Kingston. By then it was too late for me to do anything without bringing the heat down all over me big time. I even told my own father to stand down when he got wind of it and came to me about it in Jamaica. Okay, so I screwed up. This comeback tomorrow night and the tour, it's a whole new beginning for me. I've kept my own game stone clean. I can't let something like this mess up my gig after all the work I've put into coming back. That's why I called the cab and skipped out on my wife and went to see that damn drummer. The more I thought about it, the crazier I got. But can we keep this thing low key? Why do I have to be a part of it, just because I blew my cool tonight? I just got caught up in the middle of this thing."

"I said not to worry," said Rosa. "See, the reason we know you're not part of this is because Eddie is working for us."

The lines of Johnny's face hardened.

"Eddie was working for the DEA? Whoa, now."

"We busted him on a small potatoes weed deal two weeks before he was supposed to leave with your band for Jamaica," said Delahant. "Eddie's a two-time loser, in case you didn't know. He had to deal hard and he knew it, so he volunteered that Libra was planning to run in the coke. Our agreement with Eddie was that our people would stake him out after he got back from Jamaica. He would make contact with Libra and we would follow Eddie to the drop-off point and make the bust."

"That's what Eddie meant," said Madison. "He said something about being under the gun. When I got to his place, he was hiding behind the door. He looked like a guy who was in over his head and knew it."

"The punk's working a triple-cross," said Delahant. "Santini is where the real money is. He must have got word to Santini. That's why Pete sent his crew and grabbed the singer. Eddie's trying to auction the stuff off."

"And we're being obliging," said Rosa, "because we've got to warn Eddie before someone kills him. When guys with guns start showing up at his door, Eddie must know he's in way over his head. He's a junkie musician who got into small-time dealing to feed his habit. But he's got that cocaine and he's got to do something with it. If we get to him first, we can still use him to bust Libra and Santini."

"Yeah, that's why we're so damn obliging," said Delahant. "We figure you might know where Eddie took off to."

"I hate to say it," said Madison, "but I don't have a clue. How about you, Johnny?"

Johnny shook his head, no. "Eddie was a loner. It was all business between me and him. He was my drummer. He was a good drummer, but that was it. I don't know where he'd go. You've got to believe me."

Rosa stroked his jowls thoughtfully.

"We've got to trust the both of you. Maybe you're right and we should have blown the operation and busted into Santini's to get you out. So let's say that's why the two of you are getting this briefing." He said to Madison, "So now that you know, I'd advise you to drop it." And he added, for Johnny, "Wouldn't want anything to happen to my daughter's favorite singer."

"Don't you worry about that, my man," said Johnny. "This here is your mess, and you're welcome to it."

"One word of warning," said Delahant to Madison via the rearview mirror. "You've made a powerful enemy tonight in Santini, but watch out for this Libra, too. If he thinks Johnny was in it with Eddie, then there is more trouble coming your way until we find Eddie. Ever hear of Ice Crusher, real name Leon Bowman?"

"That's the murder your partner was talking about. He was going to be the biggest thing in rap and hip-hop, and they said he had crossover potential. Until he and some woman were killed in a recording studio."

"Libra ordered that hit," said Rosa. "Ice Crusher was a small time pimp and crack dealer who knew how to rhyme and remake himself and smooth out the rough edges. You know how drugs and the rappers go hand in hand."

"Sad but true," said Johnny, mostly to himself.

"He was Libra's first choice to make the connect that he finally got Eddie to make. Ice Crusher's brain must have been a block of ice. Libra tried him out on a small-time audition deal, and the punk tried to rip Libra off. That's why he was capped."

"Them drugs don't lead to nothing but the poor house or the morgue," said Johnny in a cadence of musical lyricism.

"We'll keep the lid on your involvement in this as best we can," Rosa told Johnny. He looked at Madison. "Now, you fellas continue driving back to town and forget any of this ever happened. Me and Delahant will handle things from here on out."

Delahant confirmed that the briefing was over with a curt, "Thanks for your cooperation."

Rosa stepped out of the Buick, opened the back door on Johnny's side and held it open solicitously while Johnny and Madison debarked.

Madison and Johnny returned to the Corolla. The drizzling mist felt good after the confines of the car. He brought the engine to life and drove off, leaving the agents' darkened car behind with Rosa standing beside it, watching them go.

CHAPTER SEVEN

Madison drove in silence.

They reached the freeway and as they were merging from the on ramp into the traffic flow, Johnny said, "Man, I sure hope you're well paid if tonight is a typical shift on you jay-oh-bee."

Madison checked their backtrack along the well-lighted freeway in the rearview mirrors. There was no sign of the Buick.

"The pay's not bad. Trying to collect it, sometimes that's another story."

Johnny laughed a full-throated laugh with the smoky timbre of his singing voice.

"Whoo-whee, did all of that just happen? This has been one crazy night." His wraparound shades turned to Madison. "I owe you, man. I don't care if it was a job. You put everything you had on the line for me. I owe you."

"Arn Shapiro will owe me when this job is done."

"You're going to think I'm an ungrateful son of a bitch."

"Go ahead," said Madison.

"Well hell, buddy." Johnny sighed one of his sighs from around the ankles. "It goes against this blind man's grain to be assigned a babysitter, you dig? I mean, I've got my people, my handlers, and my father and Lana run things for me up close and personal. Fact of the matter is, Mr. Madison, I know it ain't your fault but I resent it. I owe you for tonight. But you've got to understand that one of the hardest things about being blind is having people think

75

they've got to take care of you."

"Johnny, I've been called in to help out guys with twenty-twenty vision who were twice your size, okay? It's not about you being blind. It's about your jay-oh-bee. Your job is to play the music. Mine is to take care of lice like Eddie Chase and Pete Santini and Libra."

A pause as Johnny thought that over. Then he nodded.

"You're right. Okay, Steve Madison, you take care of the bad guys and I'll kick it tomorrow night at Kiel Auditorium."

Madison reached over and turned on the Corolla's radio.

"Hey, Johnny. You know the airwaves in this town. Find us a good station."

Madison guided the Corolla onto the street where Johnny Willow lived.

Johnny smiled as if he could see through the dark, rainy windshield. He had been paying attention to every turn and curve made since they'd exited the expressway.

"Almost home. What a night. I'm damn glad it's over."

Madison decreased their speed. He studied Johnny.

"How much of what happened tonight do you want to get around, even to your promoter?"

"What are you saying?" Johnny reached forward to deftly mute the dash radio, which had been playing smooth jazz. "Are you telling me you'd cover up, even from Shapiro?"

"I am supposed to be working for Arn. But damn, he could have one of his ulcer attacks if I told him everything that went down."

"You mean like you having to kill a man?"

"Among other things. My point is, since Arn's the guy paying my tab, I ought to watch out for his health."

Johnny's brow furrowed while he considered what he

was hearing, and his sigh this time was of nothing but relief. He extended a hand and they exchanged a reverse handshake as if a pact were being sealed.

"I appreciate that, man. I really do. I'll tell Dad everything when we're alone, so anything you want to tell him, that's cool. But my wife, well, Lana tends to worry too much, you know the way women be. It'd help me some on the domestic front if our story was that you caught up with me, Eddie wasn't around, so we split and drove around some while you talked sense into me. How's that sound?"

"If that's the way you want it. My only job here is to make sure you're on stage tomorrow night giving the best concert you've got in you."

Johnny sensed the disapproval that Madison tried to keep out of his reply.

"Listen, bro, I love that woman with all my heart and soul. I hate the way she tears herself apart inside every time she starts worrying about me."

"We'll play it any way you want," said Madison, and he pulled into the Willow driveway, braking Carin Aucott's car and switching off the headlights and engine. "I would like one thing in return, Johnny."

"Such as what?"

"Does Eddie Chase have some dirt on you that he used as leverage to get you to go along with him smuggling in half a key of coke? It looks like getting you onstage free and clear tomorrow night means getting that little twerp out of your hair. If there is something, give me something to work with and I'll neutralize the guy."

Madison could almost feel the singer's sightless eyes narrow behind Johnny's opaque wraparound shades.

"You gave those narcs the idea that you weren't interested in Eddie anymore. That's good enough for me. I know I was a fool to go to that sucker's house with a gun in the first place, feeling crazy like I was. I say, let it be. Forget about Eddie Chase."

"Will Eddie Chase forget about you? That punk's in a real bind now. He's going to be scrambling for traveling money, what with Libra and Santini and the DEA wiring the city for him. My guess is if he does have something on you, Johnny, he'll come straight at you with it and start putting pressure on you all over again."

"I told you. I didn't want him getting caught because it was too far along and when I found out what Eddie was up to and even if I'd turned him over to the law, the connection between me and drugs . . . that's something I don't ever want to see in the tabloids or ever again in any way, shape, or form. That's all there was to it."

The front door of the Willow home flew open and light spilled across the front yard. Three figures hurried toward the car.

Inside the Corolla, Johnny touched Madison's forearm.

"So how do we stand, bro? How much are you going to tell?"

"We'll see."

They stepped from the car.

The light rain had stopped again. Patches of starlight twinkled through breaks in the low cloud ceiling.

"Johnny . . . *Johnny!*" Lana seemed to collide with her husband, a wild embrace that lifted her feet off the ground as they hugged and she planted kisses all over his face. "Oh Johnny, Johnny, we've been so worried about you. Where have you been?"

Johnny held her close, tightly.

"I'm sorry, baby."

"Oh Johnny, I'm so glad you're back. I was praying that nothing bad would happen."

Without relinquishing their embrace, Johnny seemed to peer over her shoulder at where Carin Aucott stood next to Johnny's father.

"I heard two people running up just now. Did you have a good flight in from the Coast, Carin?"

She brushed away an errant tendril of red hair, the strain lines relaxing around her green eyes and wide smile.

"Yes, Johnny. The record company thought I should be on hand for tomorrow night's concert, and so did I. So here I am. I'm scheduled to see every major radio programmer in the St. Louis area tomorrow to get your new CD even more airplay. A lot of people are going to know that you're back to stay."

Taylor Willow stepped forward to give his son and daughter-in-law a hearty one-armed embrace.

"Son, I've invited Carin to stay with us here at the house tonight." He added, to Madison, "We've got one other guest room to fill, Steve, if you'd care to stay with us."

"Thanks." Madison nodded with a grin. "Sounds great."

They strolled up the stone walkway to the house, Johnny and Lana had their arms around each other like lovers on a stroll. Carin walked alongside them. Madison and Taylor fell back in the procession. The others did not note their withdrawal. Carin and the Willows disappeared into the house, leaving Madison and Taylor alone on the porch.

"Tell me."

Madison told him, omitting nothing.

Taylor Willow listened and when the tale had been told, he exchanged a standard handshake with Madison with the same firmness of his son's grip.

"Everything you did was in Johnny's best interests. I'm

honored to offer you the hospitality of our home for what you did for my son tonight. Sometimes he's good, most of the time like when he's making his music, but he's got that dark side, sure enough."

"I'm taking Johnny at his word. He told me that he was going to give you the full lowdown first chance he got."

"I just wish those two narcs weren't messing around in this. I mean, in Johnny's private life. Especially at a time like this."

"The consensus seems to be that Eddie Chase has signed his own death warrant. He's double-crossed Libra and the DEA, and Santini wants him too. He could be dead already, and with no Eddie Chase, the narcs lose interest in Johnny and they're off our backs. They want Santini and Libra, not your son."

Taylor nodded as he listened, but the words sounded overly optimistic even to Madison's own ears.

Santini stood with Carlo, watching men load Danny's body into the back of the Cadillac.

The corpse was zippered into a Government Issue body bag. The men swung it into the trunk compartment. There was some unintelligible snickering as the trunk was slammed shut.

"Shut up," Carlo told them.

"Yeah," said Santini. "And Carlo, I want these boys to make sure Danny is never ever found. You do get me, right?"

"I get you, Mr. Santini. By tomorrow morning, Danny's body won't even exist." He barked at his men by the Cadillac. "You heard Mr. Santini. Step it up."

The men got in without another word and the driver drove off. Santini and Carlo watched the car's tail lights round the nearest corner of the house, and vanish from sight.

"I don't want it ever talked about, what happened to me tonight," said Santini. "You tell that to the boys, Carlo. What that commando guy did to me . . . you ever mention it again, I'll slap you down. You know I will."

"I know you will, sir. Don't worry. It's forgotten."

"I want to know who that guy was, who got in here and killed Danny and . . . did what he did to me. I want a name, Carlo. And I want him dead, you hear me?"

"Loud and clear, sir."

"That's real good. And I want that punk, Eddie, too. He came to us and sold out Libra. I wish we could afford to stay away from those damn drugs in the ghetto. That's one thing the old dons were right about. But that's where the action is, and I ain't about to get cut out of a fortune."

"I know what you mean, Mr. Santini. There's too many angles. We'll find Eddie, don't you worry. Junkies are too stupid to stay lost. But this guy who waltzed in here and killed Danny . . . well, he just became *numero uno* on the hit list."

"Good, Carlo. See that it gets done. Whoever he is, that guy's going to die slow. He's going to die in front of me, screaming like a woman and begging for death because it's the only way he'll stop the hurt I'm going to put on him. Oh, it'll be sweet. That one, he's going to pay like no one has ever paid. See that the word gets out, Carlo. I'm putting up a reward."

"There won't be no place he can hide," said Carlo.

"And keep an eye on the one guy who's going to give us that guy and Eddie Chase, the little weasel, and a half kilo of coke. You know who I'm talking about, right, Carlo?"

Long pause.

Santini placed a cigar in the corner of his mouth. Carlo promptly lighted the cigar.

"Uh no, sir, I guess I don't."

"That's all right. That's why I'm the boss. Johnny Willow, he's the main point of contact. You picked him up by accident tonight when you brought him here, but that boy is what this is all about. I want a crew keeping tabs on that singer and his whole damn family. We'll intercept that coke before Libra can get his hands on it; we'll get Eddie and I'll put that tough guy's head on a platter. Now get out of my sight, Carlo. Get to work. And by the way, get some more of the boys into my study. I want all that blood cleaned up."

"Yes, Mr. Santini. Anything else?"

"Yeah. Get me a whore. I need to relax."

CHAPTER EIGHT

Madison did not sleep well that night.

He was too keyed up from everything that had happened since his arrival in St. Louis. And so, in his comfortable bed in a comfortable guestroom of the Willow house, when fitful sleep came it was haunted with faces and events with no respect for sense or chronology.

There was Johnny Willow. And Lana, and Johnny's father. And Eddie Chase and his vacant-eyed teenage concert rat companion. Pete Santini filtered through the half sleep and half dream, as did a more shadowy presence that could only have been the one they called Libra. And of course Danny confronted him in his dreams, the man he had killed at Santini's mansion. But the faces that bothered his subconscious the most belonged to Rosa and Delahant . . .

Never an early riser unless it was absolutely necessary, he made it downstairs to the kitchen at nine o'clock the next morning. He had ingrained in himself the discipline of allotting a set number of sleep hours before waking. When his eyes opened, he was alert as a cat startled from a nap. At such times as he could afford, he might allow himself to sleep for seven hours, though never more. More often than not when on the job, though, he preferred to grab his sleep in four-hour increments, invariably finding this to be sufficient to replenish him.

Shafts of gold lanced in through the windows with a warming freshness that seemed to suggest that all that had happened last night could too have been nothing more than the tenacious tendrils of a dream.

He showered and dressed: jeans, western boots, a black T-shirt and a brown leather jacket to conceal the shoulder-holstered .44.

The house was quiet. These were music industry people. Night people, some or all of whom were still in bed. It had, after all, been one hell of an evening.

Walking downstairs from the second-floor guestroom, he considered Rosa and Delahant. He had not seen the last of them. He sort of liked the fatherly Rosa, and Delahant seemed competent and tough. They were willing to go along with a cover-up of Johnny's involvement in a drug smuggling situation. In return, they would now expect Madison's full cooperation in their endeavors to play their side of this deal, not his own as he was used to doing.

He would ride with the moment here in St. Louis. He would stay loose, viable. He intended to make things happen, to make his own breaks for the Willow family, and when those breaks came, he would ride them for all they were worth.

He found Carin Aucott sitting at the kitchen table. She was dressed in a full skirt and brightly colored blouse, and she looked as fresh as this new day, the way the sunlight burnished the coppery highlights of the red hair falling onto her shoulders.

She was just finishing a continental breakfast of danish and coffee. An open briefcase rested on the table beside her, and she was busy going through papers in the briefcase with a free hand, referring to different pages and jotting notes in margins.

When he stepped into the kitchen, she closed the briefcase, something she had appeared about to do anyway, and flashed him her engaging smile.

"Good morning."

"Hi, Carin."

"Looks like we're the early birds around here. There was a note on the table saying to help ourselves to whatever was in the fridge if we were the first ones up, so I dug in. I've got a real busy day ahead; doubt if I'll be slowing down again from now until after tonight's concert."

Madison helped himself to a glass of juice from the refrigerator.

"You must be one of these workaholics I've heard about, or someone who really enjoys her work."

"A little of both, I guess."

He drew up a chair across the table from her as she snapped her briefcase shut.

"Do all the artists on your company's label get this kind of personal treatment, or is Johnny something special?"

"Johnny is something very special." She seemed to consider having one more cup of coffee, made up her mind and stood up and went to the coffee machine. "For me, Johnny has always received top priority as an artist, as my company's business investment and as a friend."

"I know Johnny's bio. You and he go back a ways."

She returned to her chair, her smile nostalgic.

"We go back to the beginning, as far our careers go, before either of us had any contact with the music industry. The music was made from the heart for nothing but love in those days. When I first heard Johnny, he was the fourteen-year-old blind genius who fronted the choir in his father's church." Her green eyes were as if fixed fondly on a distant horizon. "His father objected at first when Johnny told him he wanted to record secular music. Taylor Willow had always seen his son as following in their tradition."

Madison nodded. "The Willow Brothers."

She sipped her coffee, that faraway look still in her eyes. "I always thought Mr. Willow's version of *I Surrender All* was a masterpiece."

He couldn't help the grin that he felt slide across his face. He no doubt looked dopey as hell, but he had never been able to remain neutral around beautiful women with a good taste in music.

"That was the first thing I said when I met him last night."

"Well anyway, Johnny and I prevailed. Never underestimate the persuasive power of a kid who wants to sing and a girl who's writing songs that need a voice. We did okay. We got a regional label; then things started happening."

"A lot of hot music came from this town."

"It still does. It's a town with music in the air, like Memphis or New Orleans that way. But I know what you mean. Back in the days it got started here, you had rock and roll: Chuck Berry; soul music: Ike and Tina; the blues: Albert King." Her eyes met his with enthusiasm, and the faraway look and all the work she had were temporarily forgotten. "The music that comes out of St. Louis is second to none, in my opinion. Did you know that the first blues ever copyrighted was *St. Louis Blues* by W. C. Handy, way back in nineteen-twelve? When I was growing up, this town was paradise to a white kid who loved black music. It was everywhere: in the parks, on the radio even when I was too young to go to the clubs to hear it played live. I was just a gangly redheaded kid with freckles who couldn't stop writing songs.

"Even when he was fourteen, in addition to singing gospel, Johnny could perfectly imitate any of the old school soul artists you could name: Ray Charles, Sam Cooke, Otis Redding, all of the classics. He had them *down*. I don't know why, but something just clicked inside my head the first time I heard Johnny sing. It wasn't in person. His father's Sunday morning services were broadcast over one of the local black radio stations when I was a teenager. That's how a lot of us first heard him sing. I begged my mother to take me down to one of the services and within a week of introducing myself to Johnny, I'd written especially for him and rented a broken-down studio. The rest, as they say, is history. Johnny worked at developing his own style after that, and he had seven Number One hits over the next three years and when I signed him to RockTime, I came along as part of the deal."

"I know Johnny's background. He left RockTime for awhile and signed with another major label. Now he's back on RockTime. What was that about?"

"It's happened to a lot of the greats. Johnny was going through changes. A bigger label offered him bigger bucks than we were, so he went with the big label and the big money, and he found out that the corporate suits did not understand what he was trying to do the way I did. He stopped turning out hits because of what they would and would not record and release, and of course the next law of nature is that they stopped having much interest in him, either recording or promoting. Johnny and I have always believed in his talent, and we always worked hard to give the public the best he had and nothing less. After his contract expired, he came home to the label that launched him, where he belongs."

"How's the label doing?"

She beamed like a new mother asked about her baby.

"Johnny's never sounded better. In every way—physically, mentally, practicing with his road band, playing in the studio—you name it and that man's got it. Johnny's time is *now*. It's a great CD. And to answer your question, sales and the label in general are doing great."

"You go on the radio talking like that and you're bound to sell out that concert."

"It was sold out a month ago. I have other acts, but the sky's the limit with Johnny this time around, with the world tour kicking off and a whole CD of new material."

He finished his orange juice, regretting where he next had to lead this thus far pleasant interlude.

"How much do you know about what Johnny was involved in last night, and why I'm in town?"

She had been about to rise. She remained seated, and frowned.

"Taylor and Lana opened up to me and they were very candid with me while we were waiting for you and Johnny to come back. They told me everything they knew."

"I wonder if they did." Madison found himself tugging an earlobe, and stopped. "So you know the principal players here in St. Louis, including me?"

"I believe so. You're working for Arn Shapiro." She scrutinized him with renewed keenness across the table. "Why are you asking me these questions? You sound like a detective."

"In a way, I am. Did you know the DEA was involved?"

"With last night, with Eddie Chase?" Her brow furrowed. "No, I didn't know that. Taylor and Lana said there was bad blood between Johnny and Eddie, and that's what boiled over last night. Eddie got involved in something dirty and it could all sabotage Johnny's comeback. Is that true?"

Talking was making Madison thirsty. He went to the refrigerator and poured himself another glass of juice, and helped himself to a danish.

"Two very nice DEA agents assured me that this would not get out officially. One of them has a daughter who's a Johnny fan."

"Thank God for a diversified fan base."

"Trouble is, these narcs handed me a story with holes big enough to drive a band van through. I don't know all of the things I should know to get my job done."

"Such as?" The response was not combative, but close enough.

He set the danish aside. He'd lost his appetite. He didn't like the way she was looking at him.

"Do you know Peter Santini?"

Her frown deepened. "I know who he is. My God. Is he involved? Is that who Eddie Chase was bringing that drug shipment in for?"

"That's one of the things I'm trying to determine but yeah, Santini's in this up to his mob eyeballs. By the way, were you in Jamaica with everyone else?"

She blinked.

"There's an abrupt change of subject. What do we have here, Mr. Madison, a case of Attention Deficit Disorder?"

"I don't expect you to be happy about these questions, Carin. I'm not crazy about having to ask them. But that's my job."

"It's a rotten job. Are you a rotten person, Steve?"

"I'm not this nice all the time," he conceded. "I spoke with Santini last night. He had Johnny kidnapped to try and find Eddie, who seems to be missing though I'm expecting him to turn up at any time."

She blinked a few more times. "Kidnapped? The Mafia?"

"Were you in Jamaica with the Willow family and the band?"

"No, I wasn't. I've been breaking in a new act in L.A. Why does that matter?"

"Santini told me that he had a contact in Jamaica who was watching Johnny for him. I was wondering if that contact was you."

"Well, you're honest enough." Little fires flickered in the irises of her green eyes, and her mouth tightened. "Do I look or sound like a Mafia drug runner to you?"

"No, you sound like a redhead about to get pissed off, and that's never good news. All right, Santini's contact could have been anybody: a maid, a bell boy, a local cop."

"How nice of you to consider such possibilities. Now I see why you were asking how the label was doing. I thought that was polite conversation." Her voice tightened with a heightening anger brought on by dawning awareness. "So you thought if I or the company was financially strapped, I would make arrangements with a drug addict like Eddie Chase so I could profit from a shipment of cocaine? Do you honestly think I would jeopardize Johnny's career at this time for something like that? Do I look so stupid to you, Madison?"

Oh hell, he thought. You were always in deep trouble when they started calling you by your last name.

The wall telephone rang.

They looked at each other as the wall instrument shrilled twice more. Madison was about to answer when it stopped.

A moment later, Taylor Willow's voice called down from upstairs.

"It's for you, Steve."

"Thanks," Madison called back. He stood and lifted the receiver. "I've got it."

The extension clicked.

90

A voice said, "That you, Madison?"

Madison recognized the reedy, squirrelly voice.

"It's me. What's up, Eddie?"

"Man, I've got to split town."

Madison thought of the teenage girl who had been with the drummer.

"Are you alone?"

"Hell yeah, I'm alone. Man, I'm dead in this town. I've got to get *out*. But I need me some road money."

"We might be able to work something out."

Carin remained at the kitchen table. She had reopened her briefcase. He turned his back to her, and could hear her shuffling through papers.

Chase was saying, "I need me ten thousand dollars, and you're going to get it for me, trouble man." He gulped audibly across the connection. "You can lay your hands on that kind of cash, right?"

"Maybe."

"Do it, sucker. I get the money, you get what I've got on Johnny."

"Exclusive this time? I didn't care much for that party you threw at your house last night."

"Yeah, I want to know something about that too. How did you and Johnny get out of that?"

"I'll tell you later." Madison wished like hell that Carin Aucott was not in the room, but he could not let Chase off the hook now. "But don't worry about me. I don't want to mess up your life any more than it is already. I can be on your side. And I'll buy what you have to sell."

"Okay, you're on." Chase rattled off an address, which Madison memorized. "And make sure you come alone. I got my gun. You damn well better be alone when you show up here with that money."

"Give me an hour."

Madison hung up the telephone. When he turned, Carin was again snapping shut her briefcase. Her manner suggested that she had consciously not been eavesdropping, and that her anger had been muzzled, rationalized away or otherwise submerged.

"Can I give you a lift anywhere, Steve?"

"No, thanks. I had a rental car dropped off during the night."

They left the house together via a kitchen door to the outside. In the driveway, the chrome of a blue Mustang, parked next to the Corolla in the driveway, gleamed in the sunshine.

As they each stood unlocking their car doors, she said, "So tell me, Steve. After that third degree you just gave me? Did I pass muster, or am I on the suspect short list for some dastardly crime?"

There was no amusement in her tone.

"Carin, look. I like you. You seem like a fine person. I'm just a guy working his job."

"I hope that results in this situation getting better, not worse."

"No hard feelings, I hope."

"Let me think about that."

He let her have the parting-shot last word and watched her drive away. Then he turned to the Mustang. He was looking forward to trying it out.

Lana Willow emerged from the doorway to the kitchen as he was seat-belting himself in and reaching for the ignition. There was no way of telling if she had hurried down to catch him at the last minute, or if she had been waiting until Carin drove off and she could be alone with Madison. The legs of navy blue lounging pajamas extended below the hem of a belted robe that looked homey-comfy while accentuating her figure. Last night she'd worn makeup and had been the sophisticated African American urban woman. This morning she had the natural freshness of a country girl, but the morning sunlight upon her chocolate skin highlighted the anxiety lines at the corners of her big brown eyes and her mouth.

"Steve, I need a moment of your time."

"You've got it. Good morning, Lana."

"I'm sorry. Good morning. I'm not myself this morning. Johnny tells me everything is going to be all right, but . . ." She chuckled at herself. "You know how women are. And, well, you and I haven't really had a chance to speak alone to each other since you got here. I want you to know how important it is to me personally that you succeed."

"I know that. I can see how much you love your husband."

From his vantage point inside the car, he noticed movement behind her, at a second floor window, as if someone was watching and/or trying to listen.

"Steve, I want you to let me know if I can help. I'd do anything for Johnny. *Anything.* My husband is a genius. He writes uplifting songs that have changed the way people think for the better, and that has the potential to make this a better world." She gestured to the house and property. "Johnny's talent has bought him all of this, but his talent is really all he has."

"He has you."

"And his father, and his fans. And you, Steve Madison. You seem to be the one everybody is pinning his hopes to. Promise me that nothing bad will happen."

"I promise I'll do my best," said Madison "And right now I'd better start doing it."

93

She reached in to give his forearm a squeeze with warm, strong fingers.

"May the Lord be with you."

"Thank you, Lana."

She watched him back down the driveway. She even lifted her hand in a small farewell wave, which he returned before he drove away.

She thought about Madison. What an unusual man. Compassionate, strong. Gives the impression of being a loner but somehow manages to make friends and gain trust easily when he chooses. She couldn't recall ever seeing a man take charge and straight-kick butt the way he had.

How had it become so complicated for an ambitious young woman from an upper middle class African American family? She had a B.A. in business administration and had answered an ad in the classified ads. She'd been hired as an assistant to Taylor Willow.

Things started between her and Johnny Willow the instant Taylor introduced them on her first day on the job. She'd heard Johnny's music of course. For a few years it had been impossible to live in America and not hear his music. She and Johnny fell in love at first sight, corny but true. Something about him. The sound of his voice. His touch. His hands. Johnny was so driven as an artist, yet so laid back and together as a companion.

They were married two months after they met. A month later, she discovered that Johnny—her beautiful Johnny— was a heroin addict. This began her descent into hell, the worst period of her life. The drugs, the tabloids and Johnny's ultimate clean-out. She and her husband had been through so much together, overcoming such obstacles, only for *this* to happen.

She returned to the house, wondering why she had the feeling that her future depended on what Steve Madison could accomplish on this day.

Madison had lied to Chase, telling him it would take an hour to raise ten thousand dollars, so that he could get the drop on Eddie with a minimum of hassle, well before Chase would be expecting him, before his guard was up. He would then lean on Eddie Chase. He had no intention of paying Chase for whatever it was the guy thought he was selling. Whatever it was Eddie had, was not his to sell.

The unmarked Buick, which Madison recognized from last night, had been parked across the street, a block down the street from the Willow house. The Buick quit its position and took up a daytime tracking distance, about a half block behind the Mustang, following Madison.

He could tell, even at this distance, that the driver was the only occupant in the tail car. He could not make out which narc was tracking him. Whoever it was, Rosa or Delahant, the driver did not go for subtlety but tailed the Mustang openly.

Madison connected with I-44 into the city and the Buick followed him down the ramp, pacing now at a quarter mile. Madison drove by two exits. Then he started playing games.

The mid-morning traffic was moderate but he utilized it for all it was worth, abruptly exiting the freeway, dodging up and down quiet residential streets, the Mustang's engine and tires screeching. Quick turns. Backtracking. Then he returned to the expressway. Then off. Repeat. By the fourth exit runaround, he felt certain that he'd lost the Buick. Another five miles on the freeway confirmed this.

Whoever was driving that unmarked car had been lost.

Unfortunately so had much of the hour Madison had counted on to catch Eddie Chase unprepared. Instead he would now be showing up for his meet with Chase right on time.

Madison noticed that his knuckles were white around the steering wheel.

There had been at least one telephone extension back there at the Willows' home, and there were probably more. Had anyone overheard Eddie give Madison the address for their rendezvous? There were people who could want to get their hands on whatever it was that Eddie held or thought he was holding over Johnny's head. If that happened, it could mess up this deal royally.

Johnny was a stand-up guy and all that, but he had a short-fuse temper and last night had shown how nuts he could get about Eddie.

And there was Carin Aucott. He didn't know what to make, if anything, of the manner in which she had tarried in the Willows' kitchen while he was on the phone speaking with Chase. Had that been a coincidence, had Carin remembered some last minute details to arrange in her briefcase before she left, and the phone call meant nothing to her? Or had she consciously been eavesdropping?

He exited I-44 at Kings Highway and cut north across town toward the address on Enright that Eddie Chase had given him, playing the traffic, weaving in and out of the flow, gaining as much time as he could.

CHAPTER NINE

The principal black area of St. Louis, the ghetto, is a misshapen, nine-mile-long rectangle that borders I-70 to the north and east, Goodfellow Boulevard to the west and Delmar Boulevard to the south. While there are neighborhoods of thriving commercial enterprise and restoration, much of the area is scarred and gutted. Too many street corners are blighted by open drug sales and use, by prostitution and the smell of desperation and violence. Squalor on these streets is overseen by the towering housing projects, some of which are condemned. The air pulsates to the bass-heavy boom of rap and hip-hop music.

The address Eddie Chase had given belonged to what had once been a seedy five-story tenement, but over the years the building had degenerated from seedy to downright decay. The windows on each floor were dark and without drapes and curtains, riddled with jagged holes. Some of the windows had been broken out altogether. *Condemned* signs were clearly posted, ample evidence of non-inhabitance.

Except that Eddie Chase was supposed to be up there, waiting.

Third floor rear, he'd said.

Madison steered the Mustang to a stop at the curb in front of the building. Across the street from the dilapidated tenement, an open field covered a whole city block, littered with trash. A few puddles remained here and there from last night's rain, but most of the sidewalk and street was sun-baked and dry.

The old tenement was sandwiched in at mid-block by a squat line of business fronts to either side. The sunshine emphasized the shabbiness. The businesses had been vacated long ago. The plate glass windows stared out like the blank eyes of drunks on the morning after.

Some twelve- and thirteen-year-old boys were skateboarding up and down this stretch of sidewalk. A pair of winos sat on the curb, half a block away, sharing a bottle wrapped in brown paper.

Madison stepped from the car and the faces smoothed impassively at the sight of a white man in this neighborhood. He crossed the sidewalk and entered the building.

Its front door had been padlocked once but the lock had been stolen. A hallway stretched out before him, apparently bisecting the building front to back, and ending with a flight of steps at the far end. All of the doors were open along the length of the hallway. There was about the place that eerie vibe of *nothing* except the faint, desperate buzzing of a fly trapped against a window that had miraculously managed to remain intact.

He advanced down the hallway, toward the stairs. He passed his right hand under his jacket and withdrew the Magnum. He kept close to the wall, careful to stay on the ends of the old floorboards where they would be the least likely to creak a warning to anyone who might be listening. He headed up the steps, not disturbing the stillness of the old building as he climbed.

First landing.

The buzz of the fly had been left far behind. Silence reigned in the building's interior; yet it was a sort of echoey silence. The sounds of the city could have been light years away.

He went on up, passing the second floor straight to the

98

third floor landing. He moved down this hallway.

Faded paint was peeling. Plaster had dropped down from the ceiling onto the torn carpet. There was the stench of urine. The door to the rear apartment was the one door that was closed.

Madison approached the door carefully.

"Eddie?"

Nothing.

"Eddie," louder.

Still nothing.

Positioned to one side of the door, he reached over with his free hand and twisted. The knob turned. The door opened. He gave a nudge and the wood panel swayed inward on noisy hinges. Otherwise, the silence of the building remained complete.

He stepped into the room.

His attention went first to the open doorway on the far side of the room.

A man stood in that doorway. Sunlight glared in from a window behind him. When the man moved, a ray of sunlight caught Madison right in the eyes and he couldn't discern the features, only that it was a man. And there was no mistaking the posture, or the fact that he held some sort of oversized automatic weapon in both hands, aiming it at Madison.

Madison threw himself back, out of the doorway, at the same instant that the weapon—it sounded to Madison like a silenced Mac 11 .380 machine pistol—began hammering out ugly little *spats!*

An uneven line of holes dotted the wall behind where he had stood moments before.

The gunfire had ceased.

Whoever it was in there would want out of the building now, and fast.

He heard the clamorous clanging that reverberated through the building, and was moving through the doorway again, the .44 like an extension of his clenched right fist.

There was no one waiting for him this time. A raised window sash gave onto a fire escape.

What had once been Eddie Chase was staked out spread-eagle to the posts of a bed, the only piece of furniture in the smelly, shadowy room. Eddie's dead eyes were glazed white orbs, wide with terror. His mouth had been taped shut with adhesive, but from the hideous rictus of death you could tell that he'd died screaming silently behind the tape. He had been brutally and methodically tortured.

Madison wasted no time with the dead. Sounds of the man scrambling down the fire escape were growing fainter. He ran to the window and chanced a look out.

The man had just dropped to the pavement below, from the bottom rung of the fire escape. He was looking upward, and so was his Mac 11.

Madison drew his head back inside and dodged far from the window. The silenced gunfire could not be heard up here, but the zipping projectiles ricocheted off the fire escape and masonry around the window. Bullets riddled the walls and ceiling of the room. While this volley was incoming, he charged out of the room and went racing down the stairs, taking them three at a time, rounding the second floor, landing recklessly with no slackening of speed. *He was giving time to the shooter. The guy had bought enough of a head start to escape if he had a vehicle stashed nearby.* He left the building, sprinting into the sunshine.

His rental Mustang was just peeling nosily away from the curb to the screech of burning tires and its engine roar.

The kids with their skateboards had stopped what they were doing to watch, more interested than alarmed by the firing of an automatic weapon in their neighborhood.

The Mustang shot off down the street.

Madison stalked into the center of the street. He assumed a shooter's crouch, hauling the .44 to bear on the speeding car, steadying his aim with his left wrist.

Then he lowered the gun.

The Mustang had already eaten up a block-and-a-half, and that was too far downrange to risk a noncombatant randomly wandering into his field of fire. The Mustang squealed around a corner two blocks away.

Not that much of a lead. He could still have a chance.

He straightened from his shooter's crouch and ran to where the group of youngsters was standing, watching. He reached into his back pocket, withdrew his wallet and extended a twenty-dollar bill to one of the kids holding a skateboard.

"I need to borrow that."

The kid's eyes brightened. He snatched the twenty and rolled the board toward Madison.

"Work your show, whitebread."

Madison settled his weight on his right foot upon the fiberglass board and propelled his body forward with his left foot, maintaining his balance with his elbows raised and bent, allowing for the considerable weight of the Magnum to his right side.

The clatter of the skateboard's spinning metal wheels on pavement filled his senses. He kept his body supple but was vibrating as the board jolted him along.

He steered off the sidewalk, negotiating the curb easily enough, and sped on. The breeze of his momentum rustled his hair and stung his eyes. He was really moving. There was hardly any traffic along this tenement row. He continued propelling himself with a pumping left foot.

The buildings and pedestrians on the sidewalks were starting to blur past him. He rounded the corner after the Mustang without cutting back on his speed, leaning into the turn. The shriek of the skateboard's wheels on the pavement seemed even louder than before.

And there it was.

The Mustang was stopped one block to the south by heavy cross-town traffic and a red light at the intersection of a street Madison remembered from a map as Delmar. The stop would be only seconds before the driver of the Mustang saw daylight and darted on through or into the crossflow. The driver thought he had a few seconds to play with.

As soon as he skateboarded onto the side street, Madison raised his pistol, getting close enough to risk a shot without slowing his ride on the board. He saw no vehicular or pedestrian traffic between him and the car, but he would have to use one arm for aiming since he had to keep the other arm spread outward for balance as he jarred along, and there were still too many civilians around what with drivers crossing the busy intersection ahead. Everything from a stray shot to a fatal ricochet had to be taken into account, and so he held his fire. But he was now only twenty yards from the Mustang and closing.

The driver of the Mustang must have seen him. The rental car executed a sharp righthand turn onto Delmar, causing more than one driver up ahead to stand on his brakes, filling the air with more squealing as cars on the cross-street fought to avoid collisions.

And then came the daylight he wanted.

There was a break in the traffic, and the turning Mustang was angled between Madison and another row of vacant, uninhabited lots. It was now or never before the Mustang completed that turn and rejoined the heavy traffic flow and disappeared from sight.

Madison squeezed off a round. Even speeding through the open air, the report throttled his eardrums. The skateboard lurched beneath him like a speedboat hitting turbulence. He shifted his weight, ridding the board's wobble, and the board straightened.

Ahead, the Mustang completed its turn and continued out of Madison's view, heading west . . . but moving slower than it should have under the circumstances.

He negotiated the skateboard into a turn onto Delmar with every intention of continuing pursuit for everything he and the board were worth.

But further pursuit was uncalled for.

The Mustang was stalled out a few yards from the intersection. The Magnum's heavy .44 caliber bullet had blown out the right rear tire. The car had come to a halt with its front end mounting the curb in front of an apartment building that was larger than where Eddie Chase had been killed, and twice as classy. The gunshot had drawn faces to windows, and folks who had been sitting on this building's front stoop were standing.

The Mustang was deserted.

Madison let the skateboard go rattling on its way. He advanced on the entrance of the building, but even as he eased inside, careful to stay out of the line of fire of anyone lurking inside, he sensed that the hot pursuit was over.

No one fired at him.

This carjacker had escaped.

The man could have taken any one of a dozen routes once he'd entered this building. There were three apartments, and who knew how many means of exit.

Nonetheless, Madison gave the building and its immediate vicinity a cursory search . . . and came up empty handed, as he knew he would. There was no trace of the man with the silenced Mac 11. Every apartment door was closed and most likely double- and triple-bolted. In this neighborhood, citizens would be used to huddling in their homes while violence ruled the streets around them. Even the door marked *Super* went unopened when he pounded upon it.

He reclaimed the skateboard from out front and rode it back to the condemned tenement on Enright.

A Buick was now parked at the curb where Madison's Mustang had been stolen. Delahant stood next to the vehicle, speaking into a lapel microphone. He wore plain-clothes, held a pistol, and his badge and leather credentials packet were clearly visible attached to his belt. His blond crewcut shone in the sunlight, his shiny skull almost bone-white. He and Madison were the only Caucasians in sight.

Madison coasted up to him and sent the skateboard coasting over to the kid from whom he had rented it.

"There you go, son. Thanks."

The boys were laughing, chattering excitedly to each other.

Delahant was seething. "Think you're pretty slick, don't you, Madison, losing me the way you did on those freeway exits."

"I was wondering which one of you was tailing me, you or Rosa."

Delahant indicated the direction of the room where Madison had found Eddie Chase.

"I just came down from having a look. There's a man dead up there because of you and your games. Or did you kill him?"

Madison paid attention to Delahant's gun, held downward.

"Eddie Chase wasn't much of a man, and no one I know is going to mourn his loss."

"Did you do it?"

A small crowd of street kids, winos and some prostitutes gathered, removed from the confrontation but viewing it with considerable interest.

Madison refrained from the impulse to disarm Delahant. Law enforcement was hardly an ally in his line of work, but neither were they the enemy.

"Cool off," he said. "I don't like being under surveillance and I know how to evade. Brush up on your technique."

Delahant's eyes tightened.

"Brush up on my—"

"I spoke plain. I might have made it here in time to save Chase if the DEA hadn't decided to play it cute. Last night you and Rosa led me and Johnny to believe that we were in the clear on this. But you had Johnny's house under surveillance this morning, and you had his house phone tapped."

"I've just called for backup. My partner is on his way." Delahant raised his pistol, aiming it waist high at Madison's stomach. "You're under arrest, smart guy. I'm going to put you in a world of trouble. Face the car and place your hands behind your back."

CHAPTER TEN

They released him early that afternoon.

He had been subjected to three hours plus of Q&A from a steady parade of investigators, most of them at the local level, all asking the same set of questions over and over again about what had occurred in and around that condemned tenement on Enright.

The man in charge of the investigation was a middle-aged, hard-edged Lieutenant named Garnett, who headed a special investigative task force of the St. Louis PD's Org Crime Division. Garnett pulled rank over even Homicide and, between the scene of Eddie Chase's murder and a cramped interrogation room at Headquarters, it was Garnett or one of his direct subordinates who handled the questioning.

Madison had little choice. He told them what he knew, or most of it. He left out the part about a shooting death in Peter Santini's home the preceding evening, and interestingly enough no one asked him about it. Santini had indeed taken care of that little matter in order to protect himself. It didn't do on the respectability scale to have low-rent shooters capped in your parlor. That had taken priority with Santini over getting Madison in trouble by reporting the incident.

Upon his release, he took an elevator to the busy ground floor of the lobby. Walking down the wide front steps of the police department, and away from it, he withdrew his cell phone and punched through a call.

Like it or not, it was past time for a report to the man he worked for.

The wireless connection was so crystalline, he could see Arn Shapiro's five-o'clock-shadowed face and its perennial grimace.

"Geez, Madison, I thought maybe you forgot the number. I'm paying you to keep things quiet in that town. Chasing carjackers on a skateboard. Jesus."

"You're well informed, I must say."

"Taylor Willow called me after you got yourself arrested. Arrested, yet. By the Drug Enforcement Agency. That's a real fine job of keeping Johnny out of trouble."

"Johnny got himself in trouble with a dangerous bunch of people. I came here to minimize the damage and keep him alive and well if possible."

Arn's gulp was so audible it sounded as if it came from inside Madison's head.

"Relax, Arn. I'm earning your money. I've been too busy to call. Do you want to nag, or do you want a report?"

"What've you got?"

"So you know that Eddie Chase is dead. The local cops and the DEA think they have it solved, more or less. There are two gang factions involved."

"Gang factions?"

"I was wondering how much Mr. Willow told you. Looking out for his son is his priority."

"So you tell me about the gang factions."

"The two bad guys are a local mob bigshot named Santini and a street shaker who calls himself Libra. Eddie Chase was bringing something in for Libra when the band flew home from rehearsals. I won't say more over a cell phone."

"Don't want you to. Damn this ulcer."

"When Libra gets what Eddie brought in, he intends to use the proceeds to take on Santini, who is actively engaged in an effort to short-circuit Libra before it gets started."

Shapiro made a groaning noise. "Is this as complicated as it sounds?"

"It gets worse. Eddie got himself busted by the DEA just before he left with the band for Jamaica. They squeezed him and he turned. He was supposed to set up Libra for the DEA but after he got it to the States, Eddie started playing tricks. Made contact with Santini. He started taking bids on what he had, or I should say what he had hidden somewhere."

"What do the authorities think happened to Eddie Chase?"

"A cop named Garnett is smart and tough enough to put it together. He'd like to think that Santini or Libra got hold of Eddie and tortured him for the whereabouts of what Eddie had stashed, but Garnett isn't so sure."

"He confided in you?"

"He didn't have to. He thinks there's a missing piece to the puzzle, and so do I."

"So you're telling me it could get worse?"

"I was almost killed by the guy who killed Eddie. He was waiting for me. He must have seen me drive up. I had a date with Eddie. See, that's why I *know* the cops are wrong if they think they've got this tied up."

"Explain that to me, very slowly."

"I had a date with Eddie. He was waiting for me, watching for me. That means Eddie saw his killer drive up and park in front of the tenement where he was hiding."

"Okay, I've got it." Shapiro did not sound overly pleased with his insight. "If whoever killed Eddie was a hit man for either Libra or Santini, Eddie would have seen them coming and gotten out of there while he had the time."

"And that," said Madison, "means that Eddie's killer was someone he knew. If Eddie didn't trust the person, he wasn't scared enough to run, either. That's how the killer got in close enough to do the job."

"I hope you didn't share that theory with your DEA friends."

"They're not my friends. I'll handle this like you pay me to, Arn. But there won't be any cover-ups."

"Cover-ups? Who said anything about a cover-up? I thought we were going to be careful about what was said. Jeez. I've got a feeling I still haven't heard the worst of it. How much does this have to do with Johnny?"

"I got a phone call this morning while I was at Johnny's. Did his father tell you that?"

"He did. He told me he hung up after you picked up the extension."

"It was Eddie Chase. He told me where he was, and he asked me to come over. All sorts of people could have listened in on our conversation, including the DEA. An agent tailed me when I left Johnny's. He was good, so it took awhile to lose him. I didn't know at the time that they had a tap on Johnny's line, or I would've called Eddie to warn him. I wanted a talk with Eddie. He said he had some dirt on Johnny."

"Nothing that was found with his body, I presume."

"You presume right. Either Eddie was lying and he didn't have anything to sell, or he needed the money and figured to scam it from me when I showed up. Or ambush me, the little weasel. If he did have something incriminating against Johnny, then his killer has it, along with knowledge of where Eddie stashed his shipment." Madison heard himself emit a sigh that was more resignation than weariness. "Maybe," he concluded.

Shapiro growled like a cranky grizzly bear. "Well, that's just dandy."

"What with the DEA and the local task force shuttling me between them, I picked up a few things during the handovers. One of the narcs is a guy named Rosa. They split up outside the Willow house when Delahant tailed me. Rosa continued surveillance, and he saw Johnny and Lana drive off, in a car driven by Lana, a few minutes after I left. Rosa followed them to within a half mile of where Eddie was, then he lost them."

"He lost them? Delahant lost you? Some narcs."

"It wasn't their day. I got part of it from Rosa. He says he spent a while trying to find the Willows before he gave up and gambled that they were heading to see Eddie too. That's when he got Delahant's call for backup, and that's when I was placed under arrest."

"Great job, Steve. Really great. And what about Johnny and Lana?"

"Presently unaccounted for. The nice men who gave me the once-over twice would like to see Mr. and Mrs. Willow next."

Shapiro nearly ruptured Madison's eardrum with an exasperated expulsion of breath across the long distance connection.

"Are you telling me that Johnny and Lana Willow are under suspicion of murder? Steve, that's crazy and you know it. Johnny and Lana are good, decent people."

"I'm sure a lawyer would make a terrific defense out of that. All I'm saying is that Johnny is directly involved. He went after Eddie last night and he went after Eddie this morning, and now Eddie's dead. Things like that make law enforcement people suspicious. I'll do my best to keep it from the media but as for the law, it's way too late for a cover-up."

"All right already. What about the stuff Eddie Chase brought in? Who has it now?"

"I don't know. Maybe the person who killed Eddie, maybe not."

"There's that word again. Maybe, maybe. I wouldn't suppose there's a clue as to what Eddie was using to squeeze Johnny?"

"Not yet. I'll keep you posted, Arn. I'm getting back to work."

"Don't hang up on me, dammit. I've got news for you, too. I was saving it. Get back over to the Willow place ASAP."

"I was planning to. What's the news?"

"It's Lana. Johnny got to the house about noon, Mr. Willow said. It sounds like no one's tumbled to it yet because the cops and the DEA have been so busy with you and Eddie Chase."

Madison felt his gut tighten.

"What about Lana?"

"She's been kidnapped. That's the news. And Johnny says he's not playing the concert tonight unless we find her."

Garnett stood at his office window. He watched the man, speaking on a cell phone, leave the steps of the headquarters building and join the pedestrian flow on the sidewalk several stories below. Madison was soon lost to his line of vision.

"I wonder who the hell he's talking to?"

Garnett was in shirtsleeves. He was a barrel-chested man, no more than thirty years old but with eyes that were much older after eight years on the St. Louis metro force. His face was pockmarked from a childhood disease. The flush of his complexion indicated high blood pressure.

Delahant and Rosa stood beside him.

Rosa finished slurping the coffee he'd been nursing from a paper cup.

"His boss, would be my guess."

"A man like Madison doesn't have a boss," said Delahant. "He's working for Shapiro, but Madison has maverick written all over him. I wish we had more on the guy."

They turned back to the office, a cramped cubicle dominated by a desk, with metal chairs and a file cabinet. Maps of the city were tacked to the walls.

Rosa crumpled the empty paper cup, tossed it into a wastebasket.

"We've got what we need. There were black holes in the guy's b.g.," he explained to Garnett. "That boy Madison has got himself some sort of history and no mistake. Based on what we could get with our clearance, I'd say he's lived a couple of lifetimes. There are skeletons in that man's closet. And buried bodies."

Garnett frowned. "He buries bodies in a closet? What the hell are you guys talking about? I thought we were leaning on Madison to get what we can on Libra and Santini."

"We're talking about his military service," said Delahant. "He was a Ranger. Secret operations. Most of his file is classified even to us, and we're a government agency."

"A dangerous cat," Rosa added. "A commando. A jungle fighter. That's all we need to know about Madison. And he's loose in our jungle." He turned abruptly to Garnett. "Thanks for your cooperation, Lieutenant."

Delahant nodded agreement. "Damn straight. It's always good to avoid interagency rivalry."

Garnett waved the compliments aside with a modest gesture.

"It's a fair trade. We want to take down the same people. You think Libra is a means to an end, to busting Santini? Fair enough. My people have been trying to nail Libra big time since he made it big time. We knew about his deal with Eddie. That's why you guys came to me."

Delahant perched on the corner of Garnett's desk.

"So help us out, why don't you? Any idea where Eddie could have stashed that shipment he brought in?"

Garnett sat in his desk chair.

"No idea. I do think we're close to bringing down Libra and Santini, though. Or this whole thing could blow up in our face. It seems we have a handle on all of the players except one."

Delahant nodded.

"Madison."

Rosa returned to the window, staring after the direction taken by the man they had just been interrogating.

"You've got that right, fellas. However this thing goes down—and it's going to go down fast now—when the walls start shaking, Steve Madison will be the catalyst."

Sylvio's was on the fringe of the inner city, where most of the buildings were in shabby condition but the people came in more ethnic varieties.

Automotive and pedestrian traffic going past *Sylvio's* was a rich ethnic stew. Low riders passed Saabs and Porsches as well as city busses and delivery trucks. The flow of pedestrian traffic on the sidewalk was multi-racial.

A second floor apartment directly above *Sylvio's* was hazy with drifting clouds of tobacco and reefer smoke.

Libra sat, slouched in an armchair, with a sawed-off pump shotgun across his knees. He wore an Atlanta Falcons jersey and diamond encrusted dog tags, black nylon slacks and Nike sneakers. He was six-three and possessed the build of a basketball player. His eyes were heavily lidded and his front tooth was crowned with miniature golden scales.

A mountain of muscle lazed nearby on a couch. Spooner lowered the cell phone he'd been using.

"That was the runner you told me to plant across from the cop shop. Beanspot was the only thug I could get down there fast enough."

Angel, lithe and dapper, leaned against the wall in a corner. He worked at his fingernails with the nine-inch blade of a slim Italian knife.

"Beanspot's no thug. He's a loser."

Libra drew himself up in his chair.

"Quit squabbling like a pair of ho's. Where is Madison? I want to know what he knows, and then I want him *dead*."

Spooner's scarred face avoided Libra's eyes.

"Beanspot lost him."

Angel snickered.

Libra burst from his chair. The barrel of the shotgun made a short arc, connecting with the side of Angel's head. Angel staggered, hugging the wall, not dropping or making another sound.

Libra paced to a window, to stare down at the street scene below.

"I told you I can't think with bitching going on around me."

The street sounds were muted by the rhythmic rumbling of rap music, from the bar downstairs, that rattled the floorboards.

Spooner shifted to a sitting position on the couch.

"Why is this chump Madison so important? I thought it was the damn cocaine we're after. He ain't no smuggler."

"He knows more than we do," said Libra. "I want his information, and I want him out of the way."

Angel held a crimson-stained silk handkerchief to his ear, pretending not to have just been whipped upside the head with a shotgun barrel.

"I know what's important. Santini's making the streets melt, his people are putting on so much heat. There's fifty grand in it for who brings the boss Madison's head in a bag. The guy must have done something real bad to Santini, you know what I mean."

Libra turned to face them.

"Damn musicians. We cap that punk Ice Crusher for crossing me, and now this."

Spooner's cell phone beeped.

He answered, said "yeah" a few times, then "stay on the ho." Then he ended the connection.

"That was Scattershot. He was at his station, selling, when a white girl comes up to him to score."

Libra set down the shotgun. He slipped into an ankle-length leather slicker.

"Tell me what I need to know."

"The white girl was Eddie Chase's ho. That fat little blonde he's been running with."

"She could know where Eddie put the junk."

Libra headed for the door, concealing the shotgun in a special holster in his coat's lining.

"You call that nigger back. You tell him if he loses her, I'll kill him myself. Heel, dogs."

They scampered to catch up with him.

CHAPTER ELEVEN

The car rental people were not too happy about one of their new Mustangs being impounded by the police in a murder investigation. They declined to have further dealings with Madison.

He could not blame them, but he naturally avoided mentioning any of this to a competing rental agency and five minutes later he was back on the road in a late-model Mustang. He'd liked the way the previous Mustang handled, and this one was identical.

He drove in the direction of the address Arn Shapiro had given him before they'd terminated their cell phone conversation.

He had the car's FM tuned to an oldies station. They were playing some righteous tunes, and it would have been an okay drive through the streets of St. Louis except for the fact that his head was filled with questions without answers, while trying to make sense of the pieces that comprised this St. Louis jigsaw puzzle.

There were far too many variables and unknowns.

Who killed Eddie Chase?

Where was the shipment of drugs Eddie had smuggled in from Jamaica?

What blackmail dirt did Eddie have on Johnny, and did someone else—such as the killer—now have it? Did such "dirt" even exist?

And where was Lana Willow?

It was times like this when his mind could not help but

drift back however fleetingly to what he left behind whenever he took on these jobs for Shapiro.

Colorado. Beautiful Colorado. Paradise on earth.

Right. But it had to be paid for.

He exited the freeway for the final approach to the
Willow residence.

He could appreciate Shapiro's distress over the present
situation. He was paying Madison to prevent or minimize
situations that endangered multimillion-dollar acts, which
is exactly what was happening with Johnny Willow's threatening not to play tonight's concert, the all-important comeback gig after an extended "vacation." A no-show
reputation had finished many an otherwise fine star in the
past and it could happen to Johnny if he didn't go on as
scheduled tonight. Instead of launching his comeback, tonight could launch Johnny's final slide into commercial and
personal oblivion.

These jobs for Shapiro paid for life in Durango in more
ways than one.

There was the money, sure.

But though he spoke these thoughts to no one, Madison
had grown comfortable with his peacetime soldier niche as
a warrior who stood at the gates of the garden of contem-
plation, that "place" where the artistic soul of the thinker
and the teacher reflects so as to present to the collective
consciousness the truths of existence through the media of
music, acting, writing or whatever form through which the
muse of humankind seeks to express itself. Barbarians like
Libra and Santini and Eddie Chase could not be allowed to
endanger this "garden." They offended his sensibilities.

To appreciate his times of peace, a man had to feel that
he'd earned such times, and it was aiding in the elimination of
such cannibals from the music scene—sometimes temporarily,

sometimes permanently—that gave Madison's life its meaning and purpose.

And this one was personal, more than usual.

He liked Lana Willow. He liked her a lot. Shapiro was right about her and Johnny being decent people.

Thinking about it made Madison's stomach cramp into a cold knot of impatience.

At Madison's knock, Taylor Willow opened the door of the "safe house" condo. He wore a powder blue suit, a white shirt and a conservative black tie. He stepped aside for Madison to enter.

"Praise the Lord you're here. I hope something gets done now. Madison, I swear, the Devil's been at work here while you've been gone."

Johnny sat on the couch that faced the front door. He wore white knit jogging pants, sneakers and a white cotton ribbed tank top under a black cashmere felt midcalf coat. A crucifix on a thin silver chain decorated his throat. There was a half-finished bottle of beer at his feet.

"Dad, you're not in the pulpit." From behind wrap-around shades, sightless eyes seemed to burn holes where Madison stood. "So he finally makes it in, my dog who's supposed to fix everything and make it run smooth so I can do my show tonight." The words were mildly slurred.

Taylor sent Madison a pained look, then said, "Johnny—"

Johnny got to his feet, bristling.

"I thought you were sent here to take care of things, man. Now they've got my *wife*. Lord have mercy, they've got Lana."

"Tell me what happened."

Willow senior said, "They curbed Johnny's car. Lana and Johnny were coming home from a drive. A vehicle

118

came up on them before they knew it."

"They jumped out of their car and dragged her out," said Johnny. "And there wasn't nothing I could do about it. I knew about where we were. I called Dad on my cell phone and he came and got me." He reached for his beer. Madison stepped over and scooped the bottle away. Johnny knew what was happening. "Hey!"

Madison handed the bottle to Taylor.

"Pour that down the sink, will you, Reverend?"

"Glad to."

Taylor crossed to the kitchen.

Johnny glowered. "I won't be treated like a child."

Taylor called over, "Then stop acting like one."

Madison said, "You're staying sober for the show tonight, Johnny."

"I already told them—"

"I know. Arn told me. You won't play until you know Lana is safe. You know what's at stake here, Johnny?"

"Damn straight. Lana's life."

"Johnny, I'll make a deal with you. I'll see to it that your wife is safe before showtime."

Taylor returned from the kitchen.

"What sort of a performer are you, son? I taught you better, I know I did. It's about the people who come to hear you, son. You *never* let them down. You *never* do not perform unless you are physically unable."

Johnny sagged back onto the couch with another of his deep-down sighs.

"I'll think about it. Lord, I'm so balled up with worry about Lana."

"We all are, son. She'll be all right, like Steve says."

"Well she ain't all right now." He lifted his face in Madison's direction. "You've got to do something."

119

"Could you tell how many there were when they snatched her?"

"Three. They were professionals, I could tell that much. I used my piece on them."

"Think you hit anything?"

"No. I fired high. I didn't want to hit Lana or some by-stander. I just thought the surprise of me opening fire would shake things up and give her a chance to break for it. Should have saved my ammo."

"This drive you were coming back from. Where did Lana drive you to?"

Johnny waved an arm angrily.

"What's that got to do with anything?"

"Where were you and Lana driving back from when those guys jumped you? The police are looking for you." Madison's gaze took in Johnny and Taylor. "The both of you know that, or you'd be at home waiting for news of Lana, not hiding out here."

He looked around at the airy, well-appointed condo.

Taylor cleared his throat. "This is what is called a 'safe house' in those TV shows I like to watch. We keep it for when Johnny needs to get away. You know how artists are."

Madison turned to Johnny.

"Rosa says he followed you and Lana to within a few blocks of where Eddie Chase was killed."

A ponderous silence ensued.

Taylor cleared his throat again.

"Johnny, we have to clear the air. We should be working with Steve, not against him."

"Against me?" said Madison.

Johnny thought for a moment, then he said, "So what do you need me to corroborate for if a narc was following us?

120

Lana was driving me downtown for a visit with Eddie."

Madison resisted the urge to take a swing at the guy, reminding himself that it would be bad form to punch out a blind man.

"Didn't last night teach you anything?"

"Guess not."

"You listened in on an extension when Eddie gave me directions, and left right after I did. What did Eddie have on you?" Madison asked Johnny. "You wanted to get it back, whatever it is."

Johnny grunted. "He never had nothing on me. It's what I told you before. You want to know how he got me to let him come back through customs with me knowing that junk was in his drum equipment? All he did was *threaten* to tell them I was in on it if he got caught. He knew what that would do to my 'comeback.' It would be over tonight before the stage lights go on. That's why I hunted him down last night, and why I wanted to see him today. We needed to have us a serious discussion, that boy and me. But no, he didn't have nothing on me. That was just talk."

"You went looking for him both times with a gun."

Madison scratched the back of his neck, thinking.

"So Lana drove you to where Eddie Chase was waiting for me. What about Rosa? Did you realize he was following you? Did Lana try to lose him?"

"I guess we lost him by accident. Lana didn't say anything about anyone following us."

"What happened next?"

Johnny hit the arm of the couch with his fist.

"I don't know. We drove up to the address. Lana said she didn't see any sign of you either, Madison. What happened to you?"

"Mine is a long story. Tell yours."

"Okay. It happened like this. Lana was just about to park when she said some guy came running from around the side of the building, like there was someone after him. She said he had a gun. He ran right in front of our car, and Lana said that he kept looking over his shoulder."

"Did she describe him?"

"Shoot, no. We'd been arguing about me demanding that she drive me to see Eddie in the first place. I was just taking a chance that I'd get there first. I got crazy thinking about it this morning, like I did last night."

Taylor placed a hand on his son's shoulder.

"I've been praying for your deliverance from that short fuse of yours for a long time, son."

Johnny touched his father's hand with his own.

"I don't know why I'm so damn bullheaded. If what I did is responsible for anything happening to Lana, I don't know what I'll do."

"Lord have mercy," said Taylor softly.

"Stop it, you two," said Madison. "Tell me what happened next."

Johnny chuckled without humor.

"The guy with a gun changed everything. Lana wasn't making him up just to discourage me. I could tell from her voice. So we drove away and started to drive back home and that's when those men jumped us and they got Lana."

"Any word yet from whoever kidnapped her?"

Taylor nodded.

"A few minutes ago. They left a message, and the number is one of those pre-paid cell phones. I had to call them; they couldn't reach us here. No one can, not even Carin."

Madison had been too busy to think about the pretty, redheaded music exec. And thinking about her now made him frown, because he recalled again that she too had known he was on his way to meet Eddie Chase before he was delayed and someone killed Eddie.

"Has Carin left any messages?"

"No," said Taylor. "I don't have Carin Aucott's schedule, but I know she's been busy and on the move all day." He stared down at Johnny. "Her being so busy promoting tonight's show."

"Tell me what the kidnappers said."

"They've got her." Johnny slumped, morose. "They want to know where the cocaine is, or she gets hurt bad. They think Eddie delivered, and I've got possession of it."

"Did they I.D. themselves?"

"No. They want me to have time to think about it, then they'll call back. They put Lana on." His expression hardened. "They did something to her, I don't know what. Then they disconnected while she was still screaming." His words became a whisper.

"I'll kill the man who touched her."

"Son—" Willow started to say, then he seemed not to know what to say. He turned to Madison. "Do you have any idea who could have done it?"

Madison started to tug an earlobe, stopped, and then commenced tugging it furiously.

"Done what? If you mean who kidnapped Lana, my guess would be Santini. That's his m.o., right? He wants what he thinks Johnny has. He snatched Johnny last night to try and get at that shipment of cocaine. That didn't work out, so why wouldn't he try the same thing today with Lana? But if you mean who killed Eddie Chase, that's something I'm still working on."

Johnny drew his delicately fingered hands into bony fists.

"You think I'm lying, don't you?"

Madison left his earlobe alone.

"Not particularly. I just wonder how much you keep leaving out."

Taylor drew himself erect as if preparing to deliver a sermon.

"You don't think Johnny killed that low life? If that's your idea of working *for* Shapiro—"

The ringing of a cell phone interrupted him.

The facial similarity between the Willows, father and son, was made more obvious by their matching expressions of surprise.

Johnny drew forward where he sat as if ready to bolt.

"I thought you said no one could find us here."

Taylor picked up the phone, glanced at the caller I.D. readout.

"We can't do this alone, son. Arn Shapiro has a vested interest in setting this mess right, and we've got to trust him." He handed the phone to Madison. "It's Shapiro. I'm guessing he wants to know if we've heard from you."

Madison took the phone, verified that it was Shapiro's number on the readout, and answered.

"Hello, Arn."

"Well, I guess that answers my first question." Shapiro's voice carried a peculiar excitement. "You three are to-gether?"

"We're in the same place at the same time, if that's what you mean. I'm busy. What's up?"

"You're going to be more busy. I just had a call for-warded to me from the office in New York. Minutes ago, in fact."

"Where are you calling from now, by the way? I thought you were flying into St. Louis today."

"I am. I'm still in Denver tying up some loose ends after

last night's show here. Don't worry, I'll be there by tonight. Now do you want to hear about this conversation I just had or what?"

"Let's hear it."

"Someone there in St. Louis wants to make contact with you but doesn't know how to go about it. She said she saw you briefly last night, if I understood what she was saying. She wasn't exactly coherent. Sort of overwrought. She called my office because we handle Johnny and you're working for us."

"She?"

Madison was aware that the Willows were behind him, listening.

"Says her name is Heather," said Shapiro. "Heather Brown. She said I should tell you that she was the girl last night at Eddie Chase's house."

"Okay, hold it." Madison was thinking of the phone tap by the DEA on the Willow family phone line. Why wouldn't they be eavesdropping on this cell phone? "I need to get to another phone, Arn. I'll get back to you in a few minutes." He disconnected and returned the phone to Taylor. "Things are happening. I've got to be on my way."

Johnny rose from the couch.

"Steve, wait. Uh, I'm sorry about those things I said when you came in. I'm restless as all get-out. Take me with you, man. I've *got* to be a part of getting my wife back."

"Johnny, I'll tell you straight. Believe it. You'd be way out of your league, just like Eddie was. I'm on my way to get something that could give us the handle we need to get Lana back."

"The cocaine?"

Taylor made a rasping sound.

"Drugs. The work of Satan."

"Whoever kidnapped Lana thinks Johnny was a willing partner with Eddie in the smuggling deal," said Madison. "They expect us to trade the drugs for Lana."

"I'll kill the bastards," said Johnny. "I'll kill them."

His father stepped forward.

"Johnny, stop that talk."

"I have a lead on the drugs," said Madison. "I'm hoping to get my hands on that stash; then we'll meet the terms of whoever has Lana and make the trade, the drugs for your wife."

"My wife is being held prisoner by a bunch of drug hoods," said Johnny, "and all I'm supposed to do is sit and wait?" His fists were clenched tighter than before. His lower lip quivered with emotion. "You'd better be as good as they say, Madison. Yeah, you sure better be."

Johnny turned and stalked out of the room with the agility of a seeing man.

Taylor saw Madison to the door.

"I have to be honest and tell you, Steve, that a big part of me sides with Johnny on this. I'm beginning to wonder if it was a mistake for Shapiro to bring you in."

"I figured every part of you sides with Johnny. You seem like that kind of a father."

"I love Lana, too," said Taylor, "as much as if she were my own daughter, not just my daughter-in-law. I don't want to see anything bad happen to either one of those kids."

"That makes two of us," said Madison. "For now, keep an eye on Johnny and don't let him leave on his own. And keep working on him to play that gig tonight, no matter what."

"No matter what." The grave lines in Taylor's expression deepened. "That doesn't sound too optimistic."

"I'm not an optimist or a pessimist," said Madison. "I'm a realist. I'll be in touch."

And he was gone.

CHAPTER TWELVE

"She knows where the half kilo is and she wants to make a deal," said Shapiro. Madison stood at a public pay phone booth at a gas station four blocks from the Willows' condo. "She said she's taking your advice and going home to her parents. But she needs money to get out of town."

"That was the same song Eddie was singing, except he was trying to gouge a little more with a phony blackmail scam. At least she's talking the real deal."

"She says she'll be waiting for you at four o'clock at the northwest corner of the parking lot of a shopping mall called Westport Plaza at the intersection of I-270 and Page. She'll be driving a white Honda Civic."

Madison glanced at a wall clock beyond the gas station's plate glass window.

"That's twenty minutes from now. I'd better travel."

"Steve, can we trust this girl? This could be a trap of some kind. You've been tangling with some tough types back there."

"About the girl, I don't know. Maybe whoever killed Eddie didn't find out where he'd hid the shipment. Maybe he died without talking, but he told his girl while he was busy giving everyone the runaround. There's only one way to find out. I've got to make contact with her. Goodbye, Arn."

He pronged the receiver, left the pay phone and started toward his parked Mustang. Then he stopped.

A Buick had drawn up three-quarters of a block away.

A heavyset man leaned nonchalantly against the front fender, leisurely smoking a cigarette as if he had the whole day with nothing to do.

Rosa threw away the cigarette butt when Madison walked up to him.

"You and Delahant must be changing shifts. This morning he was the one on my tail."

Rosa's eyes were not unfriendly.

"You'd better get used to us, way things are going. Cigarette?"

"No thanks. How are things going, by the way?"

Rosa lit a fresh cigarette.

"We happen to be working a major bust here, as I thought I'd explained last night. This woman you're on your way to meet. Heather. Do you want me to follow you, or should we drive together?"

"Mr. Willow and his son have the impression that his condo is a safe house that you don't know about. You had that condo under surveillance and tailed me from there."

"Welcome to the high tech information age. I'm a better shadow man than Delahant ever was."

"I'm working on something, too."

"So what? Yeah, but you don't have the muscle of the U.S. government backing you up, do you?"

The tone remained cordial but had dropped a few degrees.

"Trust me," said Madison. "Give me some room to swing. I don't need long."

"Sorry, no deals." Rosa took hurried puffs on his cigarette. "We work together, Madison. Or I bust you. I have you incarcerated and see to it that you remain there. That's not an idle threat. Look at this realistically. Look at me." He threw away the cigarette, half-smoked. "My teeth hurt.

I've got a wife with medical problems. I can't always make the mortgage payments on time, and next year I'm supposed to be sending my oldest kid to college. I'm just a guy, see? And it's my duty to locate this half kilo of junk everyone's so hot to get their hands on, and see that the stuff is used to bust Libra, Santini, or both. Now, I've been trying to cooperate with you. Why do you think we released you this afternoon?"

"Because you figured you could use me to trace that half kilo?"

"See how you are? It was because I don't think Johnny Willow has anything to do with this. Now I'm asking you to cooperate with me."

"I guess you haven't heard the news."

Rosa's brow furrowed.

"What news?"

"Someone has kidnapped Johnny's wife. I think Santini ordered it. They won't release her until they get their hands on that half kilo."

"He thinks Johnny knows where it is?"

"I'd say so. Now Heather wants to deal. With me, that is. That's why it would benefit you to cooperate with me. You get your hands on that half kilo, you may not get your big bust, but Libra will be off track and the half kilo could be used to nail Santini with a kidnapping rap. No offense to the DEA, but, uh, kidnapping is a federal offense too, right? Bigger than smuggling a half-k of blow through customs."

Rosa stroked his jowls.

"It could work that way."

"Wouldn't look too bad for you if you busted a Mafia boss for kidnapping. Look at your options. I'll make sure Santini has Lana with him when we meet to trade for her; that's when you bust him red-handed for kidnapping. To do that, we need to try and meet Heather's terms in case she's telling the truth and can deliver the stash. Or I'll just let you lock me up, the way you could if you wanted to, right?"

"Damn straight, if I wanted to." Rosa studied him. "You'd put Lana Willow's life on the line like that?"

"Try me."

Rosa nodded. "Okay. I like your style, Madison, damn you. You remind me of myself twenty-five years ago. Okay. Our top priority is getting Mrs. Willow back safely. You handle Miss Heather. I'll ride along."

"And we take it easy," said Madison. "No one is mourning Eddie Chase, but you'll understand when you see Heather. The kid's got no business being mixed up in this. She's a girl who split from home for a taste of the fast lane and ended up way over her head, if you'll pardon the mixed metaphor."

"The what?"

"I don't want anything else bad to happen to her. I want to make sure that she gets home safely too, okay?"

Rosa patted his pockets for his cigarette pack, discovered it was empty, grimaced as he crumpled and re-pocketed it.

"How many times do you want to hear me say it? I've agreed to work together with you on this. I don't want anything bad to happen to anyone. That includes this girl, Heather, and Lana and Johnny."

"I know, your daughter has all of his albums. All right, let's go. We're running late as it is."

They decided to take the Mustang.

Madison drove in a southwesterly direction on I-44, in order to link with I-270, which took them north. The suburbs began thinning out into open stretches of countryside.

After ten minutes or so, Rosa said, "Delahant is a mite

peeved about this morning, you evading him and then letting Eddie Chase's killer get away. My partner thinks you made him look bad. You've made yourself an enemy."

"I've got plenty. There's always room for one more. Delahant made himself look bad. Where is he now, by the way?"

"Around. I assume Johnny and his father are lying low? Do they appreciate that we and the local cops want to question them?"

"You keep saying you think Johnny's in the clear, so why don't we talk about Delahant?"

Rosa chortled. "You don't give up, do you, bud? He wanted to pull this job, talking to you."

"Why didn't he?"

"I pulled rank. When a man gets ticked off on assignment, like Delahant is at you, he can get careless. Then he gets dead. I don't want a dead partner."

The rush hour was drawing near. The Mustang connected with I-270. The traffic grew noticeably heavier.

Madison reached over and switched on the same FM station he had been listening to earlier. After a couple of minutes, they played a classic hit by Johnny Willow with a plug for tonight's concert. That would be Carin Aucott at work, schmoozing every station in town with that wide smile of hers and comp tickets to the show for the DJs, no doubt.

His conversation with her only a few hours ago in the Willow kitchen now seemed like a very long time ago. It was that kind of a day.

He noticed Rosa tapping his foot in time to Johnny's music. He wondered what to make of Rosa. He thought how nice it would be to turn around just once on this job and not find someone pressuring him for a piece of the action.

Westport Plaza was your typical suburban mall, a mega-conglomeration of established name stores. The far northwestern corner of the parking lot was unoccupied at this time of a workday.

Except for a white Honda Civic.

There was heavy traffic on the avenues adjacent to this corner, where Heather Brown had parked, but this lone sector of blacktop was like a private, almost tranquil island unto itself.

Madison flicked off the radio. The Mustang coasted to a stop to the left of the Honda. He looked past Rosa, into the Honda Civic.

Heather looked almost like a different person from the teenage woman-child he had encountered last night at Eddie Chase's. Last night, this petite teenager had been scared spitless. Now, her complexion was as washed out as her stringy blonde hair and she reminded him of so many other burned-out concert rats he'd encountered over the years, haunted by their wrong choices, pitiful like human scarecrows; ragged and washed out, drained.

When she saw that he was not alone, her eyes flared with panic. The Honda had been idling. She shifted into reverse and tromped the gas.

"Heather, wait."

Madison's voice was drowned out beneath the gunning of the Honda's engine. The Civic shot backwards.

He saw Heather yank on the steering wheel with both of her petite hands, angling past the Mustang's tail. The Honda chugged off determinedly.

Inside the Mustang, Rosa reached under his jacket and tugged out a .38 Police Special.

"Quick. After her."

"That's not a bad idea."

Madison swung the Mustang around, shifting straight into third, peeling out and leaving a patch of burnt rubber. The Honda, across the unoccupied expanse of parking lot, was gliding into the access curve that fed into the flow of traffic on Page. Rosa was leaning out of his side window, trying to draw a bead on the Honda with his .38.

Madison lifted his foot from the gas pedal and coasted to a stop.

"What are you doing?"

The Honda Civic was merging with the traffic, heading east.

Rosa lowered the .38 and brought it back into the car.

"We'll lose her. Move it, Madison. That's a Federal order."

Madison shifted gears and the Mustang started moving again.

"I don't take orders." They merged with the traffic on Page, five car lengths behind the Honda. "You could've killed the girl with that shot, or an innocent bystander."

"I was aiming at a rear tire. You didn't have to slow us down. I'll go up against you on any target range you care to name, sonny." His eyes tracked the Honda Civic through the windshield and traffic. "You had better not be responsible for this girl getting away."

"She won't get away."

He glided the Mustang in and out of the traffic current, maintaining tracking distance as the Honda led them east.

The white Civic connected with Lindberg, turning south.

They were in the western suburbs of St. Louis again, in the Olivette region, still some wide open spaces but more densely populated the further south they traveled. There was heavier traffic along here than on Page.

The little white car puttered along in the far right lane, almost casually, well below the posted speed limit, as if the girl was under the impression that she had lost them, that she was safe. She continued on for several more blocks, then turned onto a sedate suburban street of well-manicured lawns and upper middle class homes. She was heading on a southwesterly track, most likely taking a short cut to I-270 for her return route into the city.

Madison up shifted and floored the Mustang's accelerator.

"Okay, let's take her."

Following in the wake of her turn, the Mustang closed the distance on her before the Honda Civic made the next intersection. As the Mustang drew abreast of the traveling Honda, Madison saw that the young woman's face was a wild mask of fright and dread.

He yanked his steering wheel sharply.

There was the smash of metal against metal, and the shriek and stink of braked tires tortured across pavement. Both cars rocked to a stop, nosed in to the curb.

In the abrupt silence that followed, the only sound was the passenger side door of the Honda being kicked open.

Heather Brown catapulted from her car. She hesitated for one frightened look over her shoulder at the Mustang, then took off sprinting across the nearest front yard.

Madison and Rosa leaped out of the Mustang. Rosa's door was jammed shut from having rammed the smaller car, so he lumbered his bulk out, after Madison, from the driver's side. Madison charged after the girl.

He overtook her easily. He gripped one of her wrists and swung her about to face him.

"Heather, we just want to talk with you."

He held onto her wrist. Rosa came puffing up a slope in

134

the lawn, toward them. His gun was holstered now, but this had no calming effect on the girl.

She writhed and twisted, struggling to break free of Madison's grip. She kept looking frantically from Madison to Rosa with wide-eyed panic.

"*No!* Please. Please let me go!"

He maintained his hold of her wrist, and Rosa had just reached them, when another car—a yellow Chevy Cavalier—squealed to a stop behind the Mustang and the Honda Civic.

Faces were appearing at windows and screen doors of nearby houses, drawn by the commotion. Someone would surely be calling 911.

Two men tumbled from the Chevy even as its tires were skidding the vehicle to a halt. They were African American. Both were armed. The driver was powerfully built, over six feet tall. A front gold crown filled his mouth with reflected beams of sunlight. He was aiming a sawed-off shotgun across the Chevy's roof. The other was a hulking behemoth with a scarred face, holding a silenced Mac 11 .380 exactly like the gun that had fired on Madison at the scene of Eddie Chase's murder.

Rosa moved with surprising speed for a man of his bulk. He crouched to the side, reaching for his .38. But he was not fast enough for the man with the shotgun. Its boom obliterated the suburban tranquility. The heavy round kicked Rosa off his feet like a bowling pin. He hit the ground, rolled over a few times and when he stopped rolling, he remained motionless.

The bruiser with the machine gun pistol was tracking his weapon on Madison, who released his hold on Heather's wrist, his hand diving beneath his jacket for his gun. The girl should have kept going, but she was too fear-

135

crazed to think straight. Madison assumed a combat crouch, unleathering the .44. Then Heather was darting directly between him and the gunman and at that instant, the behemoth fired. The automatic silenced reports were identical to those of the morning.

The bullets made dull little *pop!-pop!-pop!* noises as they stitched a ragged line of holes across Heather's torso. She sprawled into a hedge.

Both gunmen were now drawing beads on Madison who had swung up his .44, wondering which gunman to shoot before the other killed him.

That was as far as he got.

They had used backup.

Someone, who had crept up behind him, swung something that connected with the back of his head, and his world went dark around him.

He pitched, face forward, onto the lawn.

CHAPTER THIRTEEN

He regained consciousness without knowing how long he'd been out. His sense of smell returned before anything else. A musty closeness wanted to implode his head. Then he thought he heard footfalls on concrete.

"Yo, Libra. He's coming around."

He couldn't move. He forced his eyelids to raise.

He was tied up, bound to a low-backed wooden chair. His legs were free. His wrists were lashed behind the back of the chair with what felt like rubberized clothesline, his body bowed so the chair's back jabbed his spine just below the shoulder blades. It was not comfortable. His head was pounding, centered at a throbbing lump of agony that told him their backup man had used an old-fashioned leather sap.

That's all it took most times even with a pro. Or was he getting rusty? All it took was one instant of too much swirling around you for one good fighter, or one little human weasel, to strike at your blind spot. That's what had happened when hell had so unexpectedly erupted on a sunny street in suburbia. Rosa and Heather had gone down, and here he was. He'd only been gotten the drop on once before. That had been a fluke, too. An informant in Bangkok set him up, and he'd been taken prisoner. He had backup that time, the only thing that had turned the tables and saved his life.

This time, he had no backup. He quelled his anger at himself. A useless emotion. *Strategize.*

He was in what appeared to be an unused warehouse, lighted by harsh fluorescent overheads. Clutter, including old crates, was stacked in corners. The Chevy Cavalier was parked by a far wall. Afternoon sunlight filtered in from small, distant windows.

Three men stood facing him.

The one who had most likely sapped him in the first place, and announced his recovery a few moments ago to the others, now stood the farthest away from Madison; a lithe guy working at his nails with the blade of a folding knife. He wore a bandage over one ear. His eyes were bright. He kept licking his lips.

A short distance away stood the mountain of muscle who had mowed down Rosa.

And facing Madison squarely, fists clenched at his hips, feet planted solidly apart, towered the man who'd driven the Chevy and used a shotgun to murder a young woman in broad daylight. He leaned in to put his face in front of Madison.

"Do you know who I am?"

Madison saw the gold crown scales design in the center of the man's smile. He steeled himself against the pain that spread out to consume his whole body.

"You're Libra. You want to know where the shipment of coke is."

As he spoke, he tugged his hands back and forth behind the chair to which he was tied, discreetly testing the play of his wrists. There was none. He had been restrained in such a position as to make it impossible to gain any sort of balance or leverage with his legs. He did establish the slightest play in the knotted clothesline binding his wrists. The cord grated and scraped at his wrists. He could feel slipperiness. His own blood. But there was some slack. He kept working

138

his wrists back and forth, hoping the movement remained imperceptible to the men before him. He could loosen the clothesline if they gave him enough time. He didn't plan beyond that. He kept his eyes on Libra.

Libra returned the stare.

"You're the white boy been going around messing into everything, ain't you?"

"Eddie Chase messed things up. Just like Ice Crusher before him. You're not real good at picking guys to run your junk, are you?"

Libra stood back and for an instant Madison was certain that he was about to be struck. Instead, Libra turned his back to him and rejoined the other two.

"You going to tell me you was talking to that ho of Eddie's about the weather? Yeah, I had my eye on her for awhile, waiting for something to shake. And you drive up. Mr. Skateboard. You were talking to the ho, and I want to know what she said. She knows where Eddie stashed what's mine. She wanted to trade for a ticket out of town."

He went on working at the clothesline that bound his wrists behind the chair. The cord was loosening but still nowhere near enough for him to tug his wrists free. He concentrated on keeping his shoulders immobile, which wasn't easy. But thus far, Libra had given no indication that he knew what Madison was up to . . . unless he was the kind of guy who enjoyed playing cat-and-mouse with a man before he killed him.

"You've got it right up to a point," he told Libra. "But that's where it ends. You killed Heather before she could tell me anything."

Libra coughed up some phlegm and spat it upon the floor near Madison's feet.

"I always was too quick on the trigger. But I got you,

139

don't I? Johnny Willow, he knows what's going down. Him and that Bible thumping papa of his. And you know what they know, don't you, Mr. Skateboard? Yeah, you're in it up to your white boy eyebrows, deeper than that dead ho I capped ever was. I'll settle for what *you* know, tough guy." He turned to the dapper one who was working his nails. "Angel, mess him up some. I'm tired of talk."

"Right," said Angel.

He folded the knife, pocketed it and withdrew a leather sap from the folds of his slicker, which he dangled from his right hand. He started forward, wired and jittery.

Madison didn't worry about keeping the movement of his wrists a secret anymore. They would expect him to struggle, to try and dodge what was coming. But the clothesline was still knotted too tightly, loosening but not nearly fast enough . . .

The giant, Spooner, and Libra observed.

Madison did not take his eyes from the advancing Angel, but he spoke past him to Libra.

"You and I could work together on this."

Angel halted directly in front of him.

"Libra said no more talk."

He swung the sap.

Madison tilted his head sideways, intending to ride with the blow, but that didn't do much good. It clipped him viciously along his left cheekbone, sending more pain flashing through his body. But his instincts were intact. His legs snapped straight out and up. The toes of his boots caught Angel right in the crotch.

Angel squealed and whirled backwards, the sap sailing from his fingers. He collapsed into a fetal ball and began making dry heaving sounds into the paved floor.

The big man started toward Madison, but Libra lifted a hand.

"Hold it, Spooner." He glanced down at Angel's retching figure, then back at Madison. "Hey, Skateboard, you know what? You just earned yourself a chance to be heard. Work together, you say."

His wrists were getting more play. *It wouldn't be long. All he needed was a little more time.*

"We could deal. There's a woman's life at stake."

Libra's eyebrows arched.

"What woman?"

"Johnny Willow's wife. Pete Santini had her kidnapped."

"What's that got to do with me?"

"Don't act like you're not interested in what Pete Santini is up to. You want the shipment for seed money to take him down and he's out to stop you. That nasty powder Eddie Chase brought in from Jamaica for you is the key to everything. Everything except me. All I want is to help the Willows."

Spooner grumbled low. "Ain't he man of the year."

Libra began stalking back and forth.

"I don't make deals with boys trying to mess up my thing. I'm taking St. Louis back from the mob and giving it to the people who live here."

The clothesline was almost there. Almost loose enough for his hands to break free. Almost.

A few feet away, Angel was composed enough to draw himself to his feet, hurling muttered curses at Madison.

"What about Eddie Chase?"

Madison tugged at the clothesline. *Come on, dammit. Loosen . . .*

"What about him? A junkie. But I didn't cap him. If I had, he would have talked and I wouldn't be wasting my time with Heather or with you."

"Just out of curiosity, who do you think did kill Eddie? If he told his killer where your shipment was, maybe the killer has it now."

Libra looked at Angel, whose hands were opening and closing as if he couldn't wait to wrap them around something and start strangling.

"Angel, do you feel like doing something to this smart tough boy?"

Angel licked his lips.

"Yeah. Let me kill him slow."

Libra studied Madison. He started advancing on Madison.

Libra said, "Before you die, Skateboard, you'll tell me everything. Angel, use your knife. Slice off his eyelids."

Angel stood in front of Madison, blocking his view of the others. He reached into a pocket and obediently withdrew the Italian knife. He flicked open the blade that shimmered like a living thing in the glare of the fluorescent overheads.

Madison leaned as far back in the chair as he could, feeling the tendons of his neck muscles almost bursting with tautness. His wrists were almost free. He closed his eyes.

The blade touched his right eyelid, the naked steel somehow hot rather than cold.

There was a gunshot. The kiss of the blade ended before any slicing could begin.

Madison's eyes flashed open.

Angel was flopping down wearing a startled expression, rivulets of blood streaming from his nose, mouth and the hole in his chest.

Two figures materialized from the semi-gloom a few yards away. It was Johnny Willow and his father. They had approached stealthily while all eyes had been on Madison, and they both held guns.

142

In that first instant of recognition, Madison was not surprised to see that it was the blind singer/musician who had fired the round that had slain Angel. Johnny would have aimed for the sound of Angel's voice.

The rubberized cord binding Madison's wrists burst free. He leaped from the chair, diving toward Angel's sprawled body.

Libra whipped back his leather slicker and produced a weapon, but not the sawed-off shotgun. Instead, he tugged out Madison's own .44 Magnum. He aimed the pistol in Madison's direction and began squeezing the trigger.

Madison was already rolling toward Angel's corpse. The bullets went whistling by, over his head, one or two of them striking Angel's body.

Spooner snapped off a burst, from his Mac 11 .380, at Johnny and Taylor, who were already diving for cover behind some crates stacked in the nearest corner.

Taylor shouted in pain and stumbled to one knee, gripping his upper thigh.

"Dad!"

Johnny sounded suddenly disoriented, but he did lower himself behind the crates an instant before Spooner triggered off another burst. Spooner's aim was high.

Johnny once again aimed and fired at sound, this time at the sound of Spooner's gunfire. The blind man's bullet slammed into Spooner's shoulder, missing any vital spots, but the impact of the bullet knocked the giant into a backstep, and he temporarily lowered his weapon.

Madison reached under Angel's trench coat and found what he was searching for, a shoulder-holstered pistol. Lying prone, using the body for cover, he aimed and triggered Angel's pistol.

The slug zapped Spooner through the bridge of his nose.

A tiny black hole appeared, and a look of total disbelief plastered itself across the scarred face. The giant took a few steps back in a dead man's walk before folding to the pavement where a murky dark pool began forming beneath him.

Madison supported himself on one knee, cautiously.

Johnny had turned his attention to his father, who was trying to prop himself up against a packing crate.

The warehouse echoed with the roar of gunfire. The stink of burnt cordite drifted in the air, irritating throat and eyes.

Madison wondered, *where's Libra?*

He saw his .44, where it had obviously been tossed aside, empty. He picked up his gun. He tossed Angel's pistol back at the dead man. He reloaded the .44 from the spare ammo pocket stitched into his jacket.

The Chevy Cavalier's engine gunned to life at the other end of the oblong structure. Tires screeched on pavement. The car rocketed forward.

Madison stood between the oncoming vehicle and the closed, high double doors of the building, and it was obvious that Libra was accelerating to full speed with every intention of ramming both the doors and Madison.

He assumed a shooting stance and squeezed off a tight cluster of rounds that pounded his eardrums and shattered the Chevy's windshield directly in front of the driver's seat. The webbing around the punctured safety glass was too dense for him to see Libra.

The car went out of control into a wild sideways skid and high-powered a blank wall, and the universe became the car's beeping horn. Libra's body must have fallen forward, weighting it.

Madison rushed across to where Johnny was steadying his wounded father.

Taylor clutched his upper outside thigh. He was wincing fiercely, but Madison was relieved to see that the wound appeared superficial despite the discomfort it was causing Willow senior.

Madison stooped and took Taylor from Johnny. Hoisting the man across his back, he straightened, holding Taylor in a fireman's carry.

"I've got your dad, Johnny. Let's get out of here before the police show up."

"What about Lana?"

"She's not here. Santini has her. Now let's go."

As they emerged from the building into the fading afternoon sunlight, Madison saw that the warehouse was in a derelict, practically deserted neighborhood of similar structures. But someone had turned in an alarm. Sirens could be heard, approaching from the north, but still far enough away to give them time to withdraw.

The conservative gray Chrysler, which Taylor had driven last night to meet Madison at the airport, was waiting for them not far away, around the nearest corner. There was no one else in sight.

"I never thought I'd be so happy to see two guys who wouldn't take my advice," said Madison. "Uh, what the hell are you doing here?"

Taylor grumbled as he was carried along.

"I let this fool kid of mine talk me into it. Like I told you at the house, I reckon I can't blame him. We couldn't get used to the idea of saving Lana's life being all in your hands."

"I guess I can understand that. I'd feel the same way."

"After you left our condo this afternoon, I saw that DEA man tailing you away from there."

Johnny moved straight to the car door on the passenger

side and opened it for them.

"It was my idea to tail him. It didn't take much arm twisting to get Dad to drive."

"We should have had a parade permit. Rosa is following me and you're following Rosa, and I was too preoccupied with meeting Heather and getting Lana back for our own good. I am getting rusty."

He bent his knees and eased Taylor into the front seat.

Taylor winced with pain.

"Lord have mercy."

Johnny closed the car door when his father was comfortably settled, and circled around the front of the car using his fingertips upon the hood to guide him. "We were too far back when the guys in that Chevy jumped you. We followed them here." He climbed into the backseat using the driver's side.

"Thanks for saving my life," said Madison.

He had a brief, jolting image of Rosa and Heather Brown dying under a hail of bullets on a suburban lawn.

He drove the Chrysler away from there, in a hurry.

CHAPTER FOURTEEN

Carin Aucott rose from having applied disinfectant and bandages to the minor gunshot wound. The bullet had nicked Taylor Willow's upper thigh.

Mr. Willow had kept his eyes open throughout the procedure. The lines of his face were taut with discomfort, but you could tell that he had born worse pain than this. He seemed acutely embarrassed in his reserved, dignified way. He wore a pair of red-and-white striped boxer shorts. He stood, somewhat awkwardly, and gingerly slipped into a terrycloth robe, which he belted around the middle.

"Thank you, Carin. It still burns like all get out, but at least I can stand and get around some on it now."

Carin set the disinfectant bottle and bandages down on a side table.

"You're lucky, Taylor. Another quarter inch to the right and you might have been crippled for life."

She wore the same full skirt and brightly colored blouse as when Madison had last seen her in the kitchen of the Willow home, before Eddie Chase and Heather Brown had been murdered and so much had gone down . . .

She did not look as if she had spent the day buzzing all over St. Louis to promote Johnny's new CD and tonight's concert. Her makeup and every strand of red hair was in place. She'd been waiting for them in her car when they returned to the condo.

It had been Madison's idea for Johnny to summon Carin on his cell phone. As the daylight hours drew to a close, things were coming to a head in this matter. Three people already dead in twenty-four hours, kidnappings, the mob, drugs, a comeback concert . . . this pressure cooker was ready to explode. He preferred to have the principals centralized. There were so many loose ends, he wanted to keep tabs on what he could.

The drapes had been drawn against the encroaching dusk.

Johnny sat in an armchair in the corner. He had discarded his shoes, and sat with his stocking feet on the chair, his arms around his knees, which were drawn to his chest, visibly tense in his world of eternal darkness, without patience for this hiatus in activity no matter how temporary or necessary it might be. He did not speak, and his expression was unreadable.

Madison had briefed Carin on the high points of the day: about Eddie Chase, about the plan for him and Rosa to meet Heather and what happened there, and about Taylor and Johnny saving his life. If she was shocked, she did not let it show.

He was reminded of Johnny's hardened reaction in the presence of death when Madison had shot the hood, Danny, last night at Santini's estate. A world of morals, values, and ethics separated the Willows and the Carin Aucotts of the world from the Santinis and the Libras. Though they now drove nice cars and lived in big houses and chose to contribute to society rather than plunder it, folks like Johnny, his father and Carin were seasoned and toughened from having risen from the same mean streets that the bad guys sought to rule.

After she had heard Madison out, Carin's eyes swung first to Johnny.

"What's that Steve said about you thinking about not performing tonight?"

Something in her tone made Johnny sit up straight.

"With everything that's going on? Are you kidding, Carin? The bandleader told me before I left the house this morning that the new drummer is all set to go. But there are a million things . . . what about Lana?"

Taylor resumed sitting on a couch. His eyes were sad.

"I thought we'd been through that, son. When there's an audience for your music—"

"Those songs are complicated arrangements. How am I supposed to stay focused? I killed a man one hour ago, and I'm supposed to create art a few hours from now? My wife is in the hands of kidnappers. I pray to God that they haven't killed her already and aren't just telling us that Lana is alive so we can get them their filthy drugs." He slammed a fist into a wall so hard, Madison was surprised he didn't tear a hole in it. "I should have listened to you down in Jamaica, Dad. I should have turned Eddie Chase over to the authorities right from the start. What happened to Lana, whatever happened to her, it's my fault."

Carin stepped beside Johnny and placed an arm across his shoulders. They were the same age, but it was a maternal gesture, and he silently bowed his forehead against her shoulder.

"No one thinks that, Johnny, so don't say it."

"I think it because it's true."

"Johnny," said Madison. "The people who buy your CD's and tickets to your shows, they're drawing strength from your art to find some truth in or escape from a harsh world full of strangers. They find sustenance in your music, Johnny. You do the same."

Carin's eyes caught Madison's gaze over Johnny's shoulder.

"And we're not going to report this to the police?"

Taylor kept shifting his weight on the couch, unable to find a comfortable position.

"Honey, we don't know who to trust. The Feds know we're here; that's what Steve told us on the way back, and look, we're still free. What about the local police, Steve?"

Madison crossed to a window and eased the drapery aside a quarter inch with an index finger.

"There's a good cop named Garnett who would love to talk with the four of us. He'd give anything to be interrogating us right now."

"If the Feds know where we are, why aren't we in custody?"

He peered out at shadows gathering in the parking lot. People were coming home from work. There was nothing that looked like a stakeout vehicle.

"The Feds had this place staked out, but they didn't share their information with the local authorities. It's a turf war between the Feds and the local cops. Happens all the time. The DEA wants credit for whatever bust goes down."

Johnny straightened from leaning on Carin and drew himself tall. It was as if physical contact with her had rejuvenated him.

"So what do we do now? How are we going to get my wife back?"

Taylor had ceased rearranging himself on the couch, but he didn't look comfortable.

"Way it looks to me, we got to keep on breaking rules and play as dirty as the ones we're up against. And we're not doing it just for us," he added to Madison. "There's lots of God-loving, decent black folk around these parts whose stomachs turn at what these pieces of garbage are doing to our part of town."

Johnny's brow furrowed.

"Santini's boys got to Eddie in that tenement and tortured him, trying to find that dope. Eddie died without telling them."

"I'm not sure," said Madison. "Eddie didn't strike me as someone who could hold up under torture. Maybe his body gave out and he died without telling his killer anything. When I saw Eddie and spoke to him on the phone, he was jacked up on the drugs. The fright and pain of torture would have sent his pulse through the roof. When the autopsy comes in, I'll put my money on him dying from heart failure."

Johnny returned to the armchair, and sank into it.

"So when that dead-ended for Santini, he came after my wife. Why can't the man get it through his head that I have no idea what Eddie did with this shipment after he got back? Lord what a mess."

Madison found himself tugging an earlobe. The hell with it, he decided. He kept on tugging.

"Libra was under the impression too that Santini's responsible for Eddie's murder. I'm not so sure."

Johnny frowned. "You said something like that once before. Is there another faction involved in this? Someone we don't know about?"

"That's what I'm thinking, and it's something we should be thinking about. Punks like Eddie have a knack for getting on people's bad side."

Johnny frowned even more. "You mean like what went down between me and him in Jamaica?"

"You did show up at Eddie's house last night, looking for him with a gun."

Taylor's physical discomfort appeared forgotten in the wave of anger that washed across his features.

"That's a hell of a way to be talking about my son, and I

just got done saving your life, mister."

"Get mad if you have to. I'm just verbalizing the possibilities, the way the cops and the Feds have. But don't worry, Johnny, you won't be their only suspect in the Eddie Chase murder." He looked at Carin. "The police would see where you could have a motive for killing Eddie, too."

"Me?" She blinked, and made a face as if Madison was insane. "I didn't even know Eddie Chase."

Madison felt like a jerk, but something had been bothering him that he had to pursue.

"Maybe not. But you knew that Eddie was a threat to Johnny. Eddie claimed to have something on him. Everyone was under that impression for awhile. Carin, why were you so interested in the phone call I got from Eddie Chase while you and I were in the Willows' kitchen this morning? You had been just heading out the door to start your publicity tour, remember? But when I took that call, you stayed behind and eavesdropped."

"Just what are you saying, Steve?" Her words dripped icicles.

"The police might think it could be worth your while to have some blackmail dirt to hold over Johnny's head. Maybe you decided to take what you thought Eddie had. You hired someone to do it for you."

"And why would I do that? I love Johnny as if he were my brother. Our careers have been entwined with our friendship from the beginning. Does that sound like something I would do?"

"You're also a music company executive. Johnny almost ruined your company once before when he signed with another label. Maybe you wanted insurance that that wouldn't happen again."

"That's terrible, for you to say something like that to

me. I was not eavesdropping on you this morning. Of course I care deeply about what happens to Johnny. From the sound of your voice when you took that call, I could tell it was something important. But I didn't know who you were talking to. How could I? I just sort of thought that if I stayed around until after you were through talking, you might have some news that could help Johnny or be good for us. But you didn't say much after you finished talking on the phone, and that was that. At least I thought so until now."

Madison stopped tugging his earlobe and scratched the back of his neck, avoiding her direct stare.

"I'm feeling like more of a jerk by the second. But there's one more thing I've got to ask."

She arched an eyebrow. "Really." She emanated chilly displeasure, but was a study in self-control.

"I'm sorry, Carin. Let's just call this an exercise in simulating the police mentality."

"Get on with it." She spoke like an executive, accustomed to issuing instructions.

"Where were you this morning, Carin, around the time Eddie was getting himself killed? I guess we're talking about your first destination after you left the Willow home, after Eddie's phone call."

"As a matter of fact, I drove halfway to the first radio station on my list, got caught in rush hour traffic on the freeway and that gave me time to slow down and think. I turned around and drove back to the Willows'. It threw my whole day out of whack, but it's what I was thinking about while you were on the telephone. I had to have a talk with Taylor."

"What about?"

"What do you think? About everything that's going on. I

realized after we spoke this morning that I needed to know more than the Willows had told me last evening. When I got there, you had left. Johnny and Lana were gone too."

"We've been through that," said Johnny.

Taylor looked like a man trying to decide which emotion to feel.

"Carin and I have known each other for a long time. I met her the day her mother brought her to my church to meet Johnny all those years ago, when she first started writing songs for Johnny. We feel like Carin is family."

She sat down beside him on the couch.

"What a nice thing to say, and what a perfect time to say it. Thank you, Taylor. That means the world to me."

Johnny stirred restlessly in his chair.

"Everything my father says is true enough. But can we save the lovefest for after we get Lana home?"

"Johnny's right," said Madison. "Let's get back on point. Carin, what about after your conversation with Taylor? Where was your first stop then?"

She speared him with her frigid stare.

"I really cannot believe that you're interrogating *me*. I made the rounds of practically every radio station in the city. I can get as many disc jockeys as you want to back me up."

"It sounds like Eddie Chase was tortured and killed during the time you were with Taylor. That means that as murder suspects, you two alibi each other."

Taylor held up a hand as if cueing a congregation to silence.

"Hold on there, son. Are you saying that the Reverend Taylor Willow is under suspicion for that junkie's murder?"

"Why shouldn't I alienate everybody and make a clean sweep of it? Johnny's your flesh and blood. You have more motivation to protect him than anyone, and Eddie Chase posed a serious threat."

Carin said, "You're loathsome, speaking to us in this way."

Johnny made an angry gesture.

"Yo, I don't want to hear any more about who killed Eddie Chase. That's good riddance to bad trash. I know full well it wasn't Carin who capped him and so do you, Madison."

"It's not going to do us any good to stick our heads in the sand," said Madison, "and pretend that the police and the Feds aren't asking themselves the same questions. I'd apologize to everyone here, but that's the way it is."

His and Carin's gaze connected for an extended moment. He tried to understand what he saw in hers, but failed. She picked up the medicine bottles and bandages.

"I'll put these away."

She left the room.

Taylor studied Madison, his countenance severe.

"What about Lana? What does all of this get us?"

Johnny nodded vigorously.

"Now you're talking. We're wasting our time on the dead. What about Lana?"

"You're right," said Madison. "That's enough alienation. There is a way we could set this up."

"What do you have in mind?" asked Johnny.

"Let's forget about who killed Eddie for the time being. As for getting Lana back, we do have something to deal with."

Taylor was watching him carefully.

"And what would that be?"

"I know what he's talking about," said Johnny. "Santini *thinks* we have the drugs. Let's use that, and let him go on thinking we have them."

Taylor shook his head, but you could tell he was considering this.

"I don't know. What happens when he finds out we're bluffing?"

"He won't," said Madison, "until it's too late for him to do anything about it. He wants that stuff so bad, he's already risked two kidnapping raps just to put the pressure on Johnny. I think we could play him without too much trouble."

Carin stepped back into the room. She'd been listening.

"Without too much trouble?" she echoed. "Hello, these guys are *Mafia*."

Johnny sighed and raised a hand to cover his eyes.

"We can't let anything happen to Lana. My poor baby."

"There's one thing I don't understand," said Carin. "Why did Santini kidnap Lana instead of Johnny, if he thinks Johnny knows where the shipment is hidden? Why didn't he kidnap Johnny?"

"Santini doesn't have a whole lot of time," said Madison. "The Feds are in town hot on his tail to bust him. He could have grabbed Johnny like he did last night, but what if Johnny was too tough to crack under torture? So he went with Plan B. I want him to think it worked. That plays to his ego. He'll believe that we have the drugs and want to do a deal. It's what he expects to happen."

There was a drawn-out hush. Taylor and Carin exchanged a meaningful glance.

Taylor said, "What'll it be, son? This has to be your choice, with Lana at risk the way she is."

Johnny prolonged the silence.

"Just swear to me that you'll be careful. Please don't let anything happen to my wife."

"I'll do my best, Johnny."

It took him two calls, posing as a police officer, before he was able to acquire Peter Santini's unlisted telephone number. Then he dialed the number.

Santini himself answered on the second ring.

"This better be good." Gravelly menace across the connection. "I don't like to be disturbed."

"You won't mind this," said Madison. "How's your bottom, Pete? Have any guns shoved up it today?"

"You! Why you ballsy son of a—"

"I'm the man who has what you've been looking for, Pete. I feel we have an almost intimate relationship, wouldn't you say that?"

"I'm going to kill you personally."

"How's about we make a deal first?"

"What kind of deal?"

"Come on. I've got what you want. You've got something we want. Someone. That kind of deal. A trade."

"I was going to let the boy sit and stew awhile longer."

"I want to talk with Lana."

Santini snickered.

There was nothing for a few moments.

Then Lana said, "Johnny?"

"In a sec. This is Steve. Are you all right, Lana?"

"Yes . . . yes, I'm okay." A quaver in the voice gave a lie to the words. "Please, is Johnny there?"

At least she's alive, thought Madison.

"Here he is. Take it easy, Lana. We'll get you back."

Johnny was at his side, and scooped the receiver from his hand.

"Lana, is that you? Are they treating you okay, baby? Yeah, we'll get you home. We're on it right now. You hang tough. I love you, baby. I—hey, wait. *Lana!*"

Johnny listened a moment more to a voice that must

have been Santini's, then he handed the receiver back to Madison. But he did not step away.

"All right, let's make our deal," said Madison to the telephone. "The lady for the coke."

Johnny stood next to Madison, listening.

Santini said, "Not so fast, pal. How do I know you've got it?"

"Because I'm the only one left. Eddie Chase is dead. His girl is dead. Libra's dead."

"Yeah, him and his boys dead as disco. I heard about that. You have anything to do with it?"

"Why don't we skip the small talk? Do we trade, or not?"

"All right, we trade. But just you and the junk, you got that? Carlo and me, we'll show up with her. But I want you showing up alone, smart guy. No tricks. No smart plays. I smell anything even a little bit funny, and Mrs. Willow gets herself a big fat hole in her head. *Capice?*"

Madison heard Lana whimper from that end of the connection.

"Tell me where and when. I'll be there."

"There's a stretch of road out near the Meramac River, north of Sunset Hills, just off 270, called Stoneywood. Take the Cragwold exit. A car with my boys will be waiting for you at the bottom of the off-ramp. They'll make sure you're traveling alone. You take Stoneywood south for a quarter mile. Watch for a dirt road leading to the right. My boys will be following you, but they'll pull back about there and let you drive on your own. You getting this?"

"I'm getting it. Sounds like I'm walking into an ambush."

"You want this woman I got here or not?"

"Okay, your boys have pulled back and I'm driving down a dark dirt road near the river."

"Stay on the dirt road. It's all open field out there. You'll see us. Carlo and me will be waiting for you with Mrs. Willow. And you'd better be carrying my coke."

"What time?"

"Seven-thirty."

"I'm leaving now. And no funny stuff from you either, Pete. I'm used to being outnumbered. I can cause plenty of damage with one .44 Magnum before your shooters take me out. And guess who'll be target number one."

Santini growled. "Just be there, and tell the nigger that Carlo says his wife is real nice, for dark meat."

Another laugh, and the connection ended.

Madison set down the receiver. Johnny had heard every word. Taylor and Carin were staring at him expectantly.

"It's set," he said. "I've got to be on my way. We need to work fast. I need a bag, preferably paper, with something wrapped in it so it looks like I've got the coke."

Johnny stalked off directly toward the kitchen with the ease of a man with twenty-twenty vision.

"I'll find something we can use."

The door chimes sounded, the normally calm sound cutting through the atmosphere, jagged and strident.

Taylor grumbled. "Now who could that be?"

Johnny paused in the archway that led to the kitchen. "Damn."

Carin was hugging herself as if against an arctic blast. Her eyes were wide and one hand was to her throat.

"What should we do?"

"I'll get it," said Madison.

He unholstered the .44 from under his jacket and crossed to the door, drawing it open with caution while he stood to the side, the gun held out of sight but ready if needed.

A pair of men stood in the doorway: Delahant, who could have doubled for a college jock, and his partner, the heavyset, Rosa.

Rosa looked well. His paternal smile was intact. He did not look like a man who had been stitched with automatic weapon fire a short time ago. He showed amusement at the surprise that must have registered in Madison's face. Rosa's smile was paternal, but everything else was pure DEA.

"What's wrong, son? You look like you've seen a ghost. Ever hear of Kevlar?"

"You must hurt like hell."

"I smart some, but they don't call them bulletproof vests for nothing. But say, did you forget we have you people bugged? What say we step inside and talk about Pete Santini, and this cocaine you claim to have."

CHAPTER FIFTEEN

The interior of the warehouse looked like a war zone.

Garnett watched the forensics team going over the Chevy Cavalier that had plowed into a wall.

The radiator had cracked, and its contents formed a pungent green pool around the car. Libra's body, already tagged and body-bagged, was stretched out on dry pavement nearby. The medical examiner's team was hard at work inspecting another pair of bodies sprawled upon the floor near an overturned chair. White-coated technicians were busy everywhere. There was the crackle of police radios and earnest conversation.

A black man in his forties, with a deeply creased face and wearing plainclothes, saw Garnett and angled toward him.

"Lieutenant. Should have known you'd show up."

Garnett nodded. "And I should have known that Libra would tank with a bullet in his head, not in a cell. Sometimes I wonder why we waste the taxpayers' money. These punks do a pretty good job of canceling each other out if we give them enough time and ammunition. What's the word from Homicide, Hugh?"

Hugh Hudson scanned the carnage.

"Pretty much what it looks like. A major fire fight. Those dead ones over there are the two we had tabbed for the Ice Crusher kill a few months back."

"Spooner and Angel. They killed a woman in that recording studio when they killed that rapper. That's why we

161

spend the money. To take these guys down before they kill other people."

"This is going to lead every news broadcast in the city and maybe go national." Hudson's tone was not enthusiastic. "You know the buzz. If it bleeds, it leads. And with three dead bangers, this story is bleeding like crazy, and it won't let up until we can provide some answers."

"Who owns this warehouse?"

"Working on that. A paper corp. A tax shelter just sitting here for when Libra needed an out-of-the-way place to deal with someone."

Garnett's eyes shifted to the body bag near the Cavalier. "Poetic justice."

"You guys in Org Crime will be asking Mr. Santini about this, I take it. There's been bad blood between the mob and Libra from the start. You've been working along those lines, haven't you, Lieutenant?"

"I have."

They watched Libra's corpse being loaded onto a gurney.

"So what are you thinking, Lieutenant? We're supposed to be sharing."

"Tell that to the DEA."

"Damn. The Feds are in this?"

"It's no fun being me," said Garnett. "Is there any physical evidence linking this to a mob hit?"

"Not yet. But hey, this just went down. You saw the neighborhood. But I've got people out checking for anyone who saw or heard anything. As if anyone would admit witnessing a triple gang kill in this town. What's your thinking, Lieutenant?"

"There's a new player in town. His name is Steve Madison."

"Never heard of him," said Hudson.

"You will. Big time."

"You think this guy Madison was involved in this?"

"That's what I'm thinking."

"So let's pull him in. Let's go to work on him, Lieutenant. Where is he?"

"That's the rub, my brother," said Garnett. "Madison has gone to ground in this town and if anyone knows where he is, it's the DEA. And they are not sharing."

Madison let Rosa and Delahant into the living room of the Willow condo, then closed the front door behind them.

Johnny, his father and Carin remained on the periphery, not sure how to respond or what was expected of them. The agents did not appear interested in them.

"I knew someone was going to show up," said Madison. He said to Delahant, "I expected you."

Rosa continued to downplay his return-from-the-dead act.

"I learned a long time ago that no well dressed agent on assignment should be without a Kevlar vest. That's how I plan to make my retirement next month. I knew a lot of good agents never made it that far."

"Good to have you back," said Madison. "So, uh, since you were eavesdropping, what do you fellas think about my 'deal' with Santini?"

"You're setting him up so we can nail him on a kidnap charge," said Rosa. "That's bigger than drugs. I'd say that's a damn good deal."

"Do you have the coke?" asked Delahant.

"Eddie Chase hid it somewhere," said Madison, "and I don't know where. His girl said she knew where it was, and I'd say the secret died with her. But that's not the way

163

Santini sees it. He has it figured that Libra tortured and murdered Eddie for that coke then I got the half kilo from Libra after I, uh, took him down."

Delahant's eyes burned with dislike.

"Were you responsible for what happened at that warehouse?"

"I had a hand in it. I'll take responsibility."

"You cool-handed bastard." Delahant spoke to Rosa. His eyes never left Madison. "Wouldn't it be funny if cool-hand here did get his hands on a small fortune worth of illicit drugs?"

Madison said, "Sounds to me like you're still stuck on how you blew it this morning when Eddie got himself killed."

"Damn you, I didn't blow any damn thing. If you hadn't—"

Rosa stepped between them.

"I don't think Madison has the drugs. He'd cooperate with us if he did. His job is to keep Johnny Willow clean. He's bluffing Santini. Yeah, Madison. My partner's right. You really are a cool-handed bastard, I'll give you that."

"The point is," said Madison, "I'm the key to your kidnap bust whether you like it or not. If you want Pete Santini tonight, caught in the act, you're going to play my game. You heard him on the phone, right? He'll have the approach staked out, and he's probably got the PD wired. He could have your license plate numbers and descriptions."

Johnny faced the agents head-on.

"You've got to go along with us on this. This is Lana's life we're talking about! Please don't do anything that will endanger her." There was more than a hint of panic in the plea.

Rosa nodded.

"You're both right." He looked at Delahant with mild rebuke. "What happened this morning to Eddie Chase was no one's fault but the killer's. Or maybe it was everyone's fault. We're all trying to play it so clever. From here on, everyone here plays it straight." He turned to Madison. "We'll use your car. I had the local cops release your Mustang after Libra and his guys whisked you off. Garnett is their Org Crime man and he sure wants to see you, but he doesn't know where to look because I assured him that me and Delahant would cover that."

Madison glanced at Johnny, Taylor and Carin.

"That's the turf war I was telling you about." He said to Delahant and Rosa, "I'll rendezvous per schedule with Santini. You two can ride on the floor of the backseat, under some blankets or something."

"Wait a minute," said Delahant.

Madison continued as if he hadn't heard.

"You can go for Santini *after* I get Lana. And you want to know the truth? It'll be better having you along."

"But Lana—" began Carin Aucott.

"Santini has no intention of letting me or Lana walk away from tonight," said Madison. "He has to kill me after the way I humiliated him at his home in front of his men, and that will make Lana a witness to my murder. But what he thinks I have will bring Santini into the open tonight, and he'll have Lana with him."

Delahant glowered. "And what about the coke? You still maintain that you don't have it and you don't know where it is?"

"I don't have it and I don't want it," said Madison. "If I had it, you'd have it."

"That's good enough for me," said Rosa. "We'll wrap something up for you to pass off, then we roll." He placed a fatherly hand on Johnny's shoulder. "And Johnny, I want you to know that the highest priority tonight is to get your wife back, safe and sound. We won't do anything that endangers her life. I swear that to you."

Taylor said, "Lord knows she's in danger right now. Doesn't look like we have much choice, son, but to cooperate with these Federal fellas."

Johnny nodded. "I understand. You men just be careful out there tonight. And thank you, each of you. Thanks."

He turned and left the room. A moment later, the lilting melody of blues piano playing could be heard.

Madison started toward the kitchen, as Johnny had before the interruption.

"I'll get something wrapped up to pass off; then let's do it."

Taylor's weathered face wore more worry than before.

"Sweet Lord, let everything work out for the best."

Carin approached Madison a few minutes later as he was about to climb in behind the steering wheel of the Mustang. The Willow condo was the last in a row, with a side entrance to a shadowy quadrant of the parking lot.

The night sky was star-studded. The air was nippy with the recent memory of winter.

Taylor stood watch. Rosa and Delahant were ensconced on the floor of the Mustang's backseat.

Carin drew Madison aside, out of earshot of the others.

"This morning in the kitchen at the Willow house, you as much as accused me of drug trafficking with Eddie Chase, and then you thought about if I was a spy in Johnny's camp for Peter Santini."

"I wasn't accusing." Madison didn't know why he sounded defensive. He'd always found himself thrown off stride when a beautiful woman was angry with him. "I was asking questions."

"A little while ago you said maybe I was blackmailing Johnny."

"I said the police might think that," said Madison. "I was asking questions. It's my job, Carin."

"Don't get patronizing with me." Her eyes and mouth were strained lines in her face. "Do you think *I* killed Eddie Chase or had something to do with it?"

"Carin, go inside and listen to Johnny play. I'll see you at his concert tonight."

"If he decides to show up. Lana is the love of Johnny's life but in another way, Johnny and I have been soul mates from the beginning. You go to hell, Madison."

He felt her eyes follow him to the Mustang.

He followed the directions Santini had given him, driving west out of St. Louis on I-44 until the suburbs dropped away altogether, replaced by wide stretches of open countryside marred only occasionally by the lights of small rural townships or random clusters of habitation. At I-270, he continued north; then he exited at the Cragwold Road off-ramp exactly as he had been told to do.

It was 7:28.

The atmosphere in the Mustang was as chilly as the air outside. Neither agent had said much during the ride.

The mob car, a black Lincoln limo, honed in on the Mustang's tail right at the bottom of the exit ramp. The two vehicles connected with Stoneywood, a meandering country road, and tracked south. There was no traffic on Stoneywood. The Lincoln held its distance at several car lengths.

Madison drove without moving his head.

"They're on schedule."

"We're sitting ducks back here," groused Delahant. "For chrissake, don't take any chances."

"Everything is a chance," said Madison.

He unleathered the Magnum from its shoulder holster under his jacket as he drove. He steered with the handgun resting on the car seat by his right thigh. He kept close tabs on the tailing headlights in his rearview mirror. He didn't see the narrow dirt road, branching off to the right, until he was almost past it. He brought the steering wheel around and the Mustang jounced across deeply rutted earth.

The Lincoln held back, not following but barring the road.

Right, thought Madison. *We're boxed in.*

He reduced his speed and drove on. The Mustang's headlights stabbed into the inky darkness ahead.

Another couple of hundred yards and the rutted back road fed onto a meadow on a rise overlooking an expanse of the Meramac River, in the distance like a silver ribbon beneath the metallic glow of a half moon. The lights of a small township shone beyond the river.

Another late model Lincoln, identical to the first, was parked south of the dirt road on higher ground.

He braked and doused the Mustang's engine and lights when he reached a point downhill and parallel to the waiting vehicle.

"This is it." He whispered as much to himself as to the men hidden in the backseat.

For once, Delahant had nothing to say.

Rosa said, "Good luck, Steve."

Madison stepped from the car. He held a loosely wrapped brown paper shopping bag at his left side. The Magnum was clearly visible in his right fist.

There was freshness to the air, a reminder of last night's rain. A breeze kicked up from the west, playing with strands of his hair.

He started up the incline toward the Lincoln.

Three people awaited him. Their silhouettes, and some of their features, were discernible in the moonlight.

Santini stood nearest to Madison, his feet planted solidly apart, hands on his hips, much as Libra had faced him in the warehouse that afternoon.

These were the parasites who thought they could take and break and rape anything they wanted that was precious and meaningful and civilized, be it a human life or something more abstract like art and the gift of creativity. These were the barbarians at the gate, mocking the good, daring the decent to try and stop them.

Madison's senses were attuned to the surrounding gloom.

The wind died. The night became still except for the crackle of crickets.

Carlo was positioned directly behind Santini. His right fist was gripped around one of Lana Willow's slender arms like a vise. His left hand was hidden beneath the lapel of his coat, obviously near a gun. Madison wondered why the bruiser thought it necessary to conceal his piece when Madison openly displayed his own gun.

Despite her predicament, Lana looked chic in a sweater-levis-boots outfit. She wasn't going anywhere, and she wasn't saying anything. She'd been gagged with a strip of duct tape. But her breathing and tensed posture bespoke an awareness that this moment was on the razor's edge between life and death.

When Madison was ten paces away, Santini's voice cracked like a whip.

"Stop right there, smart guy. Another step and Carlo blows you and the woman away."

Madison stopped. He held up the brown paper bag.

"Here's what you want. I want Lana. Let's make our trade."

Santini snarled. "Toss it halfway over. Carlo picks it up. You get the broad."

"Broad," said Madison. "Have you been hanging out with the ghost of Frank Sinatra or what?"

He tossed the parcel to the ground as directed.

Santini lifted an arm and snapped his fingers.

"Carlo."

Maintaining his hold on Lana, his left hand still out of sight beneath his coat, Carlo advanced warily, drawing Lana with him until they stood at the spot where the brown bag had landed. Carlo released Lana with a shove.

She stumbled. Carlo laughed and delivered a kick that sent her pitching down the grassy incline toward Madison.

Carlo leaned over, retrieved the parcel and rejoined Santini again. They started for the Lincoln.

Lana tumbled to Madison's feet. His eyes connected with hers for an instant. Her eyes above the tape gag were wide with rioting emotions.

He knelt down and lifted her, as he had carried Taylor from the warehouse. With his right arm still cocked at the elbow and his index finger still on the Magnum's trigger, he hurried the gagged woman back toward the security of the Mustang . . . and Rosa and Delahant, who were still secreted in the backseat.

Carlo and Santini hesitated beside the Lincoln, but did not get in. Carlo could be seen withdrawing his left hand from beneath his coat. It was now apparent why he had not displayed this "gun." It was a gun, all right, but not the kind that fired bullets. Madison identified the hardware as a standard U.S. Army issue flare launcher. Carlo aimed the pistol-like object skyward and compressed the trigger.

A flowering ball of cobalt blaze arced like a shooting star to explode with a blinding burst directly above them. The rolling expanse of meadowland became harshly etched in a brilliance that froze everything into a ghostly silver tableau.

Madison carried Lana behind the Mustang. He crouched down, lowering her next to him upon the ground beside the car.

Santini and Carlo had taken cover behind the Lincoln. They opened fire with pistols at the Mustang. Bullets punctured the Mustang's chassis.

Understandably enough, there was a commotion from within the Mustang.

"What the hell's going on?"

That was Delahant.

"We're coming out," said Rosa.

Before Madison could reply, he heard a rapid, evenly spaced, chopping airborne rumble advancing from the west.

The bubble-front helicopter banked into a holding pattern at treetop level like a genetically bloated dragonfly hovering in the harsh false daylight of the flare. Unearthly reverberations from its turbine engine and whirling blades drowned out everything else.

Madison shielded Lana's body with his own, and looked up to discern the outlines of two men up there in the helo: the pilot, and the guy in the open hatchway. The passenger was leaning out as far as he could, aiming a heavy cylindrical object downward.

The object was a flame-thrower.

CHAPTER SIXTEEN

High-powered spotlights from the hovering helicopter beamed a light harsher than the flare, highlighting Madison and Lana like a stage-light.

His first concern was the incoming fire from Carlo and Santini. He leaned an arm across the trunk of the Mustang, remaining low behind the car with Lana crouched beside him, and pegged off a spaced pattern of three rounds along the length of the Lincoln, and the incoming fire ceased.

A rear door of the Mustang burst open and Rosa and Delahant tumbled out, weapons drawn. Rosa moved with a combat grace odd for a man of his heft and age. Delahant was right behind him.

Madison motioned away from the Mustang.

"Flame thrower!" He shouted to be heard through the resounding throb of the chopper's engine and rotors. "Get away from the car!"

More gunfire from behind the Lincoln.

Madison triggered off return fire, as did Rosa and Delahant. Santini and Carlo ducked down as the volley of projectiles punched holes in their car, shattering glass.

With his left arm around Lana's waist, supporting the gagged woman, Madison rushed for a clump of boulders several yards from the Mustang.

Lana remained limber and supple, allowing herself to be physically directed, not panicky, obviously wanting to flow with whatever Madison had in mind.

He gained cover with her behind the boulders, tossing

off two more rounds at Santini and Carlo as he ran. He deposited Lana below their line of fire, though a bullet whistled by dangerously close, followed by the whine of a ricochet.

Madison snapped open the .44's cylinder and shook free the spent cartridges and reloaded from the twelve-round ammo belt at his hip. Then he peered around a boulder at the action in the meadow.

Rosa and Delahant had dived away from the Mustang as Madison told them to, in opposite directions. And just in time.

The flamethrower up in the hovering helicopter ignited with a windy *ka-thump-whooossshhh!!!* The Mustang was swallowed up in an eyeball-searing explosion that was doubled when the car's gas tank blew. The twin fireballs merged and climbed amidst billowing smoke, and when the Mustang settled, all that remained of it was a charred hulk.

The lashing tongue of flame disappeared back up into the cylindrical object like movie footage run in reverse. The chopper's rumbling noise continued to pummel the senses.

The flare was beginning to fade. The gloom was regathering. The chopper banked back and the spotlight arced away for a moment, but Madison knew that the pilot was only lining up for another pass with the flame-thrower.

Carlo and Santini opened fire with renewed vigor from behind the Lincoln, shooting at Rosa and Delahant who had been caught in the open, as well as at Madison, who resumed returning fire. He saw Rosa and Delahant doing likewise.

Delahant shouted something. He reeled about and sprawled to the ground, grasping at his shoulder.

Rosa was still on his feet and was as yet unscathed. The chopper was his primary target. He held a Mac 11 .380

173

auto pistol that chattered a steady stream of fire skyward at the chopper.

The helo kept on coming, maintaining treetop level. The man with the flame-thrower leaned further out this time from the bubble-front, preparing for another torching blast that would annihilate everyone and everything in its path.

Santini stayed where he was, firing from his well-concealed position behind the Lincoln.

Carlo stepped clear of the Lincoln for a better shot at Rosa, then instantly understood his error in judgment. He shifted his weight, swinging his .45 around, remembering Madison . . . too late. Madison fired a round that took off the top of Carlo's skull and slammed him back against the Lincoln. His big body slumped forward and rolled down the hill.

At the same instant, one of Rosa's bullets connected with some vital part of the helicopter's engine mechanism.

The engine coughed and missed once, twice, sounding very sick, then sputtered to a stop. The abrupt absolute quiet of the night seemed as deafening as the roar of rotor blades and engine had been. The helicopter's momentum sent it at a wicked angle of descent at high speed.

Everyone on the ground paused in what they were doing to watch, in expectation of the imminent impact. A second later, though, it became apparent where Fate intended the point of impact to be.

Santini screamed once, an alarmed, ghastly shriek cut short as the plummeting helicopter plowed into the Lincoln with a frightful collision of metal impacting metal and earth. It happened so fast, Santini had no time to run away. The ground shuddered. Two separate fuel tanks erupted together and two fireballs merged into one, climbing from a bonfire of fiery fingers stroking the night.

There came the sickening stench of roasting human flesh. Except for the crackling of the fire, a hush fell across the meadow.

Madison knelt beside where Lana propped herself against the boulder. He pinched hold of the tape across her mouth.

"This is going to hurt."

Her eyes were wide. The briefest nod told him to go ahead. He stripped the tape from her mouth, using a fast snapping motion. Her sepia features pulled with a spasm of pain. Then her lungs gulped in air nosily.

"Oh, my God," she managed.

He touched her shoulder.

"Stay here. It's almost over."

He left her there, and she watched him from around the side of the boulder.

Her senses were reeling. Her breath came in quick gulps. She knew that she was approaching the threshold of panic. *Stop it,* she told herself. *Stop it.*

She drew her eyes from the flaming horror in this once pristine meadow. She closed her eyes and leaned back against the rock. She had to collect herself. She forced herself to slow her rate of breathing and used what she'd learned in doing yoga, and it began to work.

I'm alive. I'm safe.

She would live to see Johnny again. It was over. No, wait. Steve Madison had told her it was *almost* over. Almost? What did *that* mean?

She couldn't help herself. She opened her eyes and peered around the side of the boulder to see what was happening.

★ ★ ★ ★ ★

Madison walked up to Rosa, who stood surveying the wreckage of the Lincoln and chopper, just as Delahant advanced, clutching his shoulder, his face drawn with pain. But Delahant's stride was steady. They grouped in a tight circle.

Rosa studied Delahant's wound with concern.

"Andy, how bad is it?"

Delahant winced.

"Hurts like hell but nothing's busted, far as I can tell." He spoke through clenched teeth. "I guess we're lucky my shoulder is the only point they scored."

To the east, from the direction of Stoneywood Road, the snapping of gunfire carried across the night, accompanied by the sounds of car engines racing.

Three sets of headlights—vehicles with rooftop flashers on and sirens blaring—came barreling down the rutted dirt road toward the meadow.

Madison and those with him returned their attention to the heap of smoldering junk that had once been two pieces of machinery.

He said to Rosa, "Good shot, bringing down that chopper."

Rosa said, "Thank Christ it's over. No coke, no arrests, but we've got Mrs. Willow back, and Santini and Libra are both out of the picture."

Delahant did not stop grimacing and gripping his shoulder, but he remained standing.

"That's two outfits in this town without bosses, running around like chickens without heads in a scramble to position themselves. Everyone will be double-crossing everyone else."

Rosa nodded with satisfaction.

176

"And that means a whole lot of snitching, and that's going to be a world of good for us."

Marked and unmarked police cruisers careened from the dirt road into the meadow, headlights and rooftop flashers slashing through clouds of swirling dust.

Madison was not surprised to learn that Rosa and Delahant had secretly arranged for their own backup.

The vehicles spewed out hard-faced men—some in uniform, some in plainclothes—all of them toting firepower; some dispersed to the wreckage of the Lincoln and helicopter, while others hurried to the formation of boulders where Lana stood. The firefight sounds from the direction of Stoneywood had ceased.

Rosa removed his belt and finished cinching it as a tourniquet about Delahant's upper arm.

"You take it easy, buddy." His eyes moved to the approaching vehicles. "Our backup's here. It's done."

"You mean it's almost done," said Madison. "What about Eddie Chase?"

Delahant's grimace of pain almost became a sneer.

"What about him? Santini or Libra capped that punk, or they ordered it done. I'd call that a closed case."

Madison shook his head.

"But it's not, Andy. It was your partner here, Rosa, who tortured and killed Eddie Chase, and he tried to kill me when I showed up on the scene."

Rosa's eyes widened.

"What the hell are you talking about?"

Madison made a gesture.

"Can it, you bastard. I'm saying you're the one, and I can prove it."

Garnett emerged from the activity around the vehicles,

issuing commands to personnel around him. His approach went unnoted by the circle formed by Madison, Rosa, and Delahant.

"You damn well better have proof," said Rosa, "and a motive."

"Motive is the easy part. Good old fashioned greed."

Garnett didn't wait for his arrival to be noted.

"Let's hear what you've got," he told Madison. He wore a DEA windbreaker and held a rifle. "And make it fast."

Madison said to Rosa, "That was quite a speech you gave me this afternoon on our way to meet Heather Brown. Right there you were telling me your motive, and neither you or I realized it at the time. Your teeth hurt, you said. You don't have the money to go to a dentist. Your wife is sick. You don't always make your house payments on time, and next year you'll be sending a kid off to college. All those money troubles, and what do you get? Next month the bureau is pushing you into a retirement you don't want after how many years of faithful service? Or maybe they weren't so faithful, I don't know. After seeing how you worked over Eddie Chase before you killed him, nothing about you would surprise me. You saw your chance to get your hands on a half kilo of powder that you could street market easy with the contacts you've made over your years with the Drug Enforcement Agency."

Delahant studied his partner with an uncertainty that erased the pain from his features.

"When Chase was getting himself killed, Rosa was tailing Johnny Willow and his wife who were on their way to Eddie's."

"That's right," said Rosa. "And stop talking about me like I'm not here."

"You act like the good father," Madison told him, "but

you tied a man to a bed and tortured him to death. At first I couldn't figure out why the guy who killed Eddie and took those shots at me would hijack and drive away in the car that *I* drove to the scene. The killer had to have come in his own wheels. But you couldn't drive away in your own car, could you, Rosa? In case you missed me with your Mac 11 and I saw you drive away, I'd recognize the Ford you were driving from last night and I'd know it was you."

"You call that proof?" said Rosa. "My friend, you have just pulled the royal screw-up of your life." Rosa turned to Garnett, who'd been listening and watching. "I hope you heard every word this lunatic just said. I'll be wanting your deposition for my lawsuit."

"Don't worry, any of you," said Garnett evenly, still working to get a handle on what was going down here. "I'm listening to every word."

"Nice try, Rosa," said Madison, "but no good. Eddie's killer has to be someone who had immediate access to his whereabouts this morning. He was doing a good job of lying low from Santini and Libra, and if either one of those guys had killed Eddie and gotten the coke, they wouldn't have been running around all day kidnapping and killing people the way they were."

"When did it start?" asked Delahant.

Rosa made an exasperated noise.

"Andy, for the love of mike. Don't you believe this crap! How many dark alleys have we been down together?"

"Screw that," said Garnett. "I don't want memory lane." He was watching the three of them. "Help me solve a murder."

Rosa snarled. "Hold on. I'm a federal agent, you small puke cop. I'll have you busted. Andy—" He started to adopt a conciliatory tone.

"Let Madison talk," said Delahant.

"Rosa hasn't been bad all along or you would have tumbled as his partner," said Madison. "But this was too much temptation for him to resist. When Eddie Chase got back from Jamaica and started double-crossing everyone in sight, Rosa saw what a beautiful, made to order setup it was. If he could get Eddie alone and force Eddie to divulge where he'd stashed that half kilo, Rosa would have enough to retire in comfort and no one would ever suspect him of the kill. Eddie, just another casualty in the Libra-Santini drug war."

There was nothing fatherly about Rosa now.

"I'd be interested as hell in hearing how you arrived at these brilliant conclusions."

"What about that?" said Garnett. "What have you got?"

"Old-time detective work, mostly," said Madison, "and process of elimination. Who knew where Eddie was hiding out, and where were they when he was murdered? Delahant was tailing me. I can vouch for his whereabouts with my own eyes. I had his car in my rearview mirror for half the trip to Eddie's, so there's no way he could have driven across town, taken the time to tie Eddie to that bed, and tortured him to death. Carin Aucott and Johnny's father, Taylor, alibi each other. They were at the Willow house. Johnny and Lana alibi each other too, plus Eddie was too squirrelly to let a blind man get the drop on him, even a man as sharp as Johnny. And if Johnny had wanted that half kilo, he could've gotten it from Chase far more easily down in Jamaica."

"So that leaves me," said Rosa.

Madison nodded. "That leaves you. The moment you got the address of Eddie's whereabouts this morning from your and Delahant's phone tap on the Willows, you dispatched Delahant to follow me."

Delahant was watching Rosa as if through eyes that had been newly installed.

"I've got it. He wanted you and me to keep each other busy playing tag long enough for you to drive across town and put the screws to Eddie." His grimace this time was bitter. "And we were very obliging."

"After you sent Delahant off to follow me," said Madison to Rosa, "you drove as fast as you could over to that tenement where Eddie was holed up, waiting for me. He would have been surprised to see you show up but he didn't figure there was really anything to worry about. He didn't run or panic because, hey, you're the law. So he let you get up close enough, expecting to you to chew him out for screwing up the Libra bust with his double plays. That's when you clubbed him and tied him to that bed and went to work on him.

"The physical evidence is that Mac 11 .380 you're toting. Ballistics will match your gun with the bullets that were fired at me in that tenement where Eddie was murdered. His killer is the one who fired at me."

"You are out of your mind." Rosa pronounced each syllable distinctly. "While Eddie Chase was being murdered, I was tailing Johnny and his wife, remember? If I wasn't following them, how did I know they were on their way to Eddie's, like they admit they were? Answer that, you bastard."

"Johnny and Lana were on their way to see Eddie," said Madison. "But you weren't tailing them. You saw them in their car in the street outside the scene of Eddie's murder, when you were running after shooting at me. Johnny says Lana tromped the brakes and told Johnny they'd barely missed running over a man who ran in the path of their car.

He was carrying a gun, and that made them change their minds about going to see Eddie. You were that man, Rosa. Lana is going to identify you. What were you going to do, make sure she caught a stray bullet out here in the meadow tonight? An unfortunate accident. Which reminds me, you already caused one woman's death today."

"I don't think I'll even dignify this crap by listening to it."

Madison said, as if he had not been interrupted, "I'm talking about Heather Brown. You were carrying a .38 then. I guess you save the Mac 11 for the heavy work, like taking down helicopters or trying to kill me."

"Madison, why are you saying this crazy stuff? One of Libra's shooters cut down that poor girl. You saw it happen."

"I'm talking about what set that in motion," said Madison. "I kept wondering why Heather went through so much effort to meet me, going so far as to call Arn Shapiro's people, but she freaks so totally when you and I show up to meet her at the shopping mall. She was expecting me. She set the time and place for the meet. But when we drove up, she panicked so bad she ended up in a crossfire and was killed. Why did she flip out when she saw you? Because she was hiding there in that tenement this morning, in a closet or something. Heather saw you kill Eddie. That's what she was going to sell me for traveling money home. She didn't have the coke. Guys involved in the drug business don't trust coke whores. That was just her come-on to me."

Garnett made a grumpy sound.

"So where is the coke this fuss has been all about?"

"Rosa can tell you that when he decides to talk," said Madison. "I'd say he left it wherever Eddie stashed the half

182

kilo until things died down and the heat was off and he could cash in on it. But all Heather had to sell me was the identity of Eddie's killer, and when she saw that killer riding next to me in my car, coming to make the rendezvous with her, she understandably went into panic mode." He concluded, speaking straight to Rosa, "That's how you're responsible for getting her killed, fatso."

Delahant said to his partner, "Rosa, give me something real if anything he's saying is wrong and I'll go to bat for you. Hell yeah, we've been through a lot. I thought you were my buddy. Don't stonewall if you're innocent."

Madison looked to where Lana was being escorted toward them by a pair of SWAT team members, stepping through the headlight beams and flashing lights of the police vehicles, coming from the direction of the boulders.

"Here comes a living eyewitness. If Lana identifies Rosa as the man who ran in front of her car this morning when she and Johnny drove up to the murder scene, then this case is closed."

Rosa started to track up the heavy auto pistol he held.

Madison executed a swift, high kick, the toe of his right boot connecting with Rosa's gun wrist, snapping it, aborting his aim.

The gun flew from Rosa's grasp. He lashed out with his other arm in a backhand swipe at Delahant that caught Delahant hard in the mouth, forcing his partner to stumble backwards into Madison and Garnett while Rosa turned and took off in a straight-ahead dash across the meadow, away from the vehicles, into the night.

Madison raised his .44, sighting down an extended arm at Rosa's fleeing figure. Garnett and Delahant were drawing their weapons, cursing.

"Rosa!" Delahant called. "Wait. Halt, dammit!"

Rosa's bulky silhouette had almost been swallowed up by the darkness. With all the personnel around, it was unlikely that he would make a clean getaway. But that chance did exist.

"Do I have to do everyone's job?" said Madison to no one in particular. He felt irritable and tired. He fired a single round, and blew one of Rosa's kneecaps right out from under him.

EPILOGUE

At Kiel Auditorium, Madison encountered no trouble in guiding himself and Lana through the layers of tight backstage security.

Lana had been through hell but had touched herself up considerably on the ride back into town, and Madison thought she looked fine. The closer they got to the backstage area, the more radiant she became.

Without difficulty they located Taylor Willow, Carin Aucott, and Arn Shapiro, where they stood in the wings, watching the concert that was just beginning.

There were thousands of dancing, whistling, shouting, appreciative people packed into the house, but there was only one heartbeat here tonight: the driving beat of the music as Johnny hit the stage running with his brand-new single release. He wore a sequined, black leather stage outfit that allowed his limber body to glide loose and free like the hungry young church singer who'd once upon a time burned to set the world on fire with his music. Johnny was that hot tonight right from the start. Half of the crowd already knew the opening song, its lyrics and arrangement, by heart, and thousands chanted along. Upbeat, dance club rhythms propelled the lyrics. The new drummer must have been a standby because he knew the arrangements perfectly.

Johnny was singing his song and playing his guitar, sweat running in rivulets down his handsome ebony face. But as Madison and Lana drew closer, Madison could sense that something was missing. It wouldn't show through the garish stage lights to the audience, but from backstage Madison thought that Johnny looked preoccupied behind his large wraparound shades. But Johnny was disciplined and the band was well rehearsed. Johnny's lyrical exhortations to *Make the Planet One* gave way to the bittersweet song of redemption and hope from the new CD, *Fade to Tomorrow*, which in turn segued effortlessly into his first eighties r&b hit, *Funky Up in Heah.*

In the wings there was much embracing and wide, elated smiles. Mr. Willow scooped his daughter-in-law into a bear hug, and his laugh of relief and happiness could be heard even above the raucous soul music from out front.

Carin Aucott's eyes met and held Madison's gaze for a moment. Watching her strained look disappear, he found himself somewhat surprised at the extent to which she appeared to have been worried about him, and at how happy she seemed to be to see him safe and unharmed.

It was obvious that they were all bursting with questions, but they would have to wait. It was useless to try and talk above the decibel level of the concert in progress.

Lana left the others and walked over to the very edge of the wings to watch her husband work. Her lithe figure swayed gracefully to the music.

If the opening numbers had been good, the concert became incendiary within beats after Johnny's bass player saw Lana. He stepped up and reported the news into the singer's ear during a keyboard solo. Johnny turned his face in the direction of where Lana and the others stood. He broke into a wide smile that made the bottom of his face into nothing but flashing white teeth. Then, with a high kick of his right leg, Johnny slashed at his guitar and promptly sent the band into the next number. Johnny's performance ignited with a fire that just hadn't been there before.

It became, as the St. Louis media raved the following day, the most powerful performance anyone could remember in Johnny Willow's career. Johnny performed like a man possessed, delivering every last ounce of his body and soul to the enthusiastic crowd that ranged from rappers and hip-hoppers to older fans who had been with Johnny from the beginning. In fact, one of the papers did a piece on the ethnic and age diversity of the crowd, and on how they danced and cheered as one, united by the music pouring from the stage. Johnny was slinging his guitar to his side and wrapping himself around the microphone stand, his passionate voice crying, gasping, shouting, screaming, caressing each successive song with skillfully modulated artistry. Then he'd rock back from the mike stand, head thrown back in bliss, dancing while his band rocked, and Johnny's fingers commenced delivering flurries of string-bending notes from high on the neck of his guitar, playing like a modern cross between Jimi Hendrix and B. B. King, inciting the crowd to an even greater intensity of response.

It was a show that those who witnessed it would never forget, a very special gift to the St. Louis fans who had first started Johnny Willow on his way. And it was a testament of love to the woman who had shared Johnny's joys and dreams and pain through all the years, good and bad, and who had now come back to him, alive, healthy and more beautiful than ever.

This is what makes it all worth it, thought Madison. The power of music, especially music like Johnny's, could transcend even the worst day-to-day problems and bring people together in a way that nothing else ever could. There was enough music in the world for everything and everyone, there for the listening and the nurturing and the healing, and Madison loved every bit of it. For tonight, in St. Louis, the barbarians, the destroyers, had been driven back. The Santinis and Libras of the world must never be allowed to step in the way of the sort of thing happening here onstage tonight.

Madison watched the band cook through another searing number and another after that. Johnny was giving the audience a taste of what he had grown up on, some close-harmony gospel that never lost the groove, and the crowd was eating it up. Trying to be as unobtrusive as he could, Madison turned from the others in the wings and made his way through the backstage shadows.

Mr. Willow, Carin, Shapiro, and Lana caught up with him as a group in the corridor leading toward the exit to the backstage loading dock. The music could still be heard out here and it was still loud but had a hollow, echoed effect that left room back here for conversation.

Like the others, Lana's face was etched with curiosity and lines of disappointment.

"Steve, you're not leaving?"

Carin nodded and seemed to want to touch Madison on the arm. At least it seemed that way to him.

"You should wait until the show's over," she pressed. "There's going to be a party afterward. I'm sure Johnny will want to thank you for everything you've done." A catch in her voice implied that she wanted to say more but not here, not in front of the others.

Madison tried to ignore an impulse to respond, to reach out to her as she was tentatively trying to reach something in him. He nodded in the direction of the concert.

"Hearing Johnny play like that is all the thanks I need. That man is going to turn this country around all over again with that music. I'm just glad I was able to ease things along."

Shapiro grunted. "Ease things along. That's a good one. And, uh, I thought I was paying you to do this." Dollar signs glimmered in Shapiro's eyes. "Uh, you're not suggesting that you'd forgo your fee this time around, I mean considering your love of Johnny's music—"

"Forget it, Arn. The two can co-exist."

Willow senior's expression was uncertain.

"But what happened tonight? What about Pete Santini?"

"Dead," Madison told them. "It's all over the local radio and TV right now."

Shapiro's money signs were replaced with a glower.

"But what about Johnny? Is he clear of this mess?"

Madison nodded, "Completely. The way it turned out, the DEA man, Rosa, killed Eddie Chase. The authorities have a nice tied-up package against him and that's the way they like it. They won't bother Johnny."

One of Johnny's stage crew approached.

"Mrs. Willow, Johnny's wondering if you would come join him onstage so he can introduce you between songs. He wants his fans to meet you. He, uh, says he needs a big kiss to keep him going for the rest of the show."

Lana beamed. "Of course. Tell Johnny I'm on my way." As the man withdrew, Lana turned to Madison. She took one of his hands in two of hers. "Steve, thank you for . . . everything." The warmth in her touch was in her words.

Then she was gone.

Taylor Willow shook Madison's hand firmly.

"If you must leave, then leave knowing that you have my heartfelt thanks also, and Johnny's. And I do believe that my son has learned something from all of this. At least I sure hope so."

Another handshake, with Willow senior offering Madison a place to stay in the Willow home anytime he was ever in St. Louis. Then Mr. Willow was gone too, favoring his wound although it didn't much seem to slow him down. Madison had already come to the conclusion that it would take a lot to slow Taylor Willow down.

Shapiro didn't offer Madison a handshake. Instead, he handed Madison a check. Madison didn't bother to glance at the check before pocketing it.

"You did a hell of a job, Steve. As usual. I thought you might be heading out right away, the way you love those mountains of yours. I've got the jet fueled and waiting for you at the hangar. You'll be home in a few hours."

"Thanks, Arn. Call me when you need me."

Shapiro grimaced. "Damn right I'll call you. I'm still pissed at the way you treated me when I went out there to visit you. Making me talk to you upside down."

Shapiro concluded the thought with a grunt and turned to stride off toward the show.

From the auditorium, a loud swell in the cheering erupted. Johnny must have brought his wife onstage.

But out here in the hallway, there was an internal struggle discernible in Carin Aucott's features as if she were struggling to find the right words to express what she felt.

"Steve, would . . . would I sound too damn honest if I were to say that I wish you weren't leaving? I—" Her eyes dropped, then rose to look directly into his eyes, and he could tell that she'd resolved her internal struggle. "I did spend some time, in between promo stops at radio stations, thinking about our conversation in the kitchen this morning. No hard feelings, Steve. You were just a damn hardworking man doing his job." She lowered her eyes self-consciously. "And the fact of the matter is, I've never met a man like you. The way you literally just flew into town and took command of a deteriorating situation, and then you set things right."

"It wasn't quite that easy."

"You did a beautiful thing, helping out a man like Johnny the way you did."

Madison thought of a warehouse, of being tied to a chair.

"Johnny was there for me when I needed him."

"Steve, could we, uh, get to know each other better? Or does that sound more cheap than direct?"

He grinned. "You've got too much class to ever sound cheap. And you're in a class by yourself. We could know each other better, and we should. But right now, I've seen too many people die in this city. I'm used to being alone, whether that's the best thing for me or not, and right now that's what I need."

"I understand. Then we will see each other again?"

He slid an arm around her waist and jerked her to him into a sudden embrace that melded every contour of her to him, and when their lips met it was a prolonged, open-mouthed tongue kiss that took both their breaths away when they finally broke for air.

He looked down into her eyes that were so close, the tips of their noses touched. "If you're ever in Durango . . ."

"And if you're ever in LA . . ." she began.

Neither invitation sounded trite. He realized that her arms had gone around him, and then her head was against his chest and the scent of her was in his nostrils.

She ended the clinch first, turning away to hurry toward the music, not letting him see her face.

He wondered if he was a fool. He wondered if he was not turning to his isolation for renewal, ready to bear the loneliness that was often the price of independence. He wondered if he had just turned away what he needed most in his life.

He pushed through the exit door, crossed the loading area crowded with trucks and personnel, and was soon out in the parking lot, alone in the night, walking toward one of Arn's waiting limos. Out here, the night was relatively quiet, almost peaceful after the energy inside the auditorium.

Madison wondered how long it would be before Arn would require his services again. There would always be troubles that needed fixing as long as there were Santinis and Libras out to victimize those on the right side of life, like the Willow family and Carin Aucott.

But for now, he had done his time. He had *earned* his time. Colorado was waiting.

He was going home.

A HIT FOR THE NEW AGE

It was a forty-minute flight aboard the chartered jet from Durango to Denver, where Shapiro had a chopper waiting. Twenty minutes later, the bubble-front was setting Madison down near the backstage entrance of the Red Rocks amphitheater in the foothills ten miles southeast of Denver.

On this Sunday afternoon, Tony Jardeen was scheduled to perform at the magnificent natural sandstone venue.

Tony Jardeen—The Rocker of His Generation, a ten-year-old *Time* story had labeled him. Tony's "generation" had been the 1990s, when Bruce Springsteen and Garth Brooks were the only solo artists who could compete with him when it came to selling out stadiums and arenas with an image that managed to be simultaneously patriotic and rebellious while conveying the feel-good energy of Beatles-era pop music.

Jardeen still had drawing power. Red Rocks' 8600 seats had sold out within hours of the tickets going on sale.

Madison dropped from the helo's side door as soon as the helicopter settled onto a landing pad. He wore Tony Lama boots, faded denim jeans, a black T-shirt and a short brown jacket. Beneath the jacket, as was his custom when working for Shapiro, he wore a short-barreled .44 Magnum in fast-draw shoulder leather. He moved at a low jog from beneath the whirling blades.

It was fifteen minutes to showtime. A guard at the backstage entrance glanced at his I.D. A nod passed him through. The scene backstage was wall-to-wall people, crackling with a crazy kind of energy.

Madison brought "excuse me's" into play and navigated his way through. He was soon approaching another security checkpoint manned by two hulking guys in Tony Jardeen T-shirts. The craziness thinned out to a more low-keyed vibe this far back. The I.D. passed him through this security check too.

The first thing he noticed back here was the high count of uniformed police officers bustling about.

He spotted Arn Shapiro, who had contacted him only hours ago at his property on the western slope of the Rockies. Shapiro stood in conversation with a khaki-clad lawman in front of a closed door that was across and two up from Tony Jardeen's dressing room, which had a star on its door.

The door where Shapiro stood was open slightly. The panel around the doorknob was splintered.

Shapiro's permanently five-o'clock-shadowed face wore a tight, worried grimace that only barely brightened at Madison's approach.

"Steve, thanks for getting here so fast." He turned to introduce the man he'd been conversing with. "Lieutenant, this is my associate, Steve Madison, the man I was telling you about. Steve, Lieutenant Kelvey, with the County Sheriff's Department. He's heading the investigation here."

Kelvey was thickset, in his mid-fifties. He scrutinized Madison.

"Did you know Kodopolous?"

"I knew of him. He's been Jardeen's agent ever since he moved Tony from the rock clubs in Detroit to a major label and the charts."

"Ever meet Kodopolous?"

Madison had expected these questions.

"No."

"How much has Shapiro told you?"

"He told me Kodopolous was murdered. Where did it happen?"

Shapiro picked up the conversational ball with a nod to the door where they were standing. "Right here. Okay to show him, Lieutenant?"

Kelvey nodded. Shapiro nudged open the damaged door. Madison looked inside.

The dressing room was cramped even without the corpse. An open briefcase and scattered sheets of paper covered a ledge. What remained of George Kodopolous was slumped on the floor in a corner. At first he looked like a man passed out drunk, but the super-agent who had masterminded his and Tony Jardeen's rise to riches and fame was not inebriated. Part of his face was blown away. The wall behind him was splotched with an ugly smear.

Arn closed the door.

Madison asked, "How much does the media and the audience know?"

"I work on a closed set," said Kelvey. "This area was sealed off as soon as the body was found. The security people swear there were no unaccounted-for faces backstage. My people are interrogating everyone involved with the show."

"Who was in the immediate vicinity when he was killed?"

"Jardeen, Shapiro, a woman who's traveling with Jardeen and the road manager on this tour, named Larry Ruggles. Ruggles claims he heard the shot and kicked the door open. It was locked from the inside. That's something we're still trying to figure. Kodopolous had the only key and we found it on him."

"I don't get it," said Madison. "Why are you telling me

all this? I have no jurisdiction in this case."

Kelvey registered the trace of a smile. "Mr. Shapiro always maintains a good working relationship with our department whenever he stages a show. He has a vested interest in what's going down here, so I'm allowing him representation. He wants you on deck in lieu of an attorney. He told me about your arrangement, how you take on assignments to keep his performers out of trouble. I told him to fly you in if he wanted to and I'd take a look."

"Had your look?"

"I have. Okay, hang around. Sniff around if you want to. Just don't get in the way of me or my people, or you're out. Clear enough?"

"Got it. Thanks, Lieutenant. I'd like to start by meeting Tony Jardeen."

"Let's see him together." They started in the direction of the star's dressing room. "So you've never met Jardeen before?"

The question was almost conversational.

Almost.

"Never had the pleasure," said Madison. "But I believe I know his traveling companion."

Her name was Carolyn Gentry.

She stood, arms folded, leaning against a wall of the dressing room. She was slim-hipped, close to Madison's height. She still wore her soft, nut-brown hair untamed and curly. She dressed with casual elegance in sandals and a blue print summer dress with a modest neckline. She still presented a vision of loveliness capable of knocking Madison's eyeballs right out of his head. Her brown eyes returned his gaze when he entered, then flicked away with an emotion he could not read.

Jardeen sat on a folding chair, tuning his guitar. He hadn't aged much in the decade since he'd first become a star. The sandy hair was tinged with a hint of gray at the temples. He wore pressed white slacks, matching jacket and an iridescent black shirt.

A redheaded, affable-looking guy in his thirties lounged on a couch. His freckled face reminded Madison of a middle-aged leprechaun.

Jardeen looked up from his guitar. Shapiro made the introductions. Jardeen extended a hand without rising, balancing the guitar on one knee.

"Thanks for flying in. George Kodopolous and I had our differences. Like, he was a womanizer like you wouldn't believe. But he was a great agent, and he was a human being. I want his killer caught. Ask any questions you want."

Shapiro nodded to the man on the couch.

"Steve, Larry Ruggles. Larry's an old friend of Tony's. They go back to high school."

Madison sized Ruggles up.

"The Lieutenant tells me the door was locked when you found the body."

Ruggles nodded. "Yeah, it was locked. How many times do I have to go through this?" His affability was an affectation that did not extend to his voice.

"How about one more time?" said Madison.

"Yeah, yeah, okay. Here's how it was. Everything was ready for the show. Tony was in a huddle with the band going over some last minute details. There wasn't anything left for me to do until showtime. So I came back here to see if Carolyn wanted to smoke some weed." He sent a sideways glance at Kelvey, who registered no response although he was listening attentively. "Uh anyway, I was passing the door when I heard the shot. It was louder than hell, even through the door. I tried the doorknob. It was locked so I kicked the door open and went in."

"Right after you heard the shot?" asked Madison.

"Yeah. Ten, maybe fifteen seconds after."

"You're a brave man, running toward the sound of gunfire."

"I wasn't thinking straight," said Ruggles. "But that's what I did."

"What did you see inside the room?"

"Hell man, you know what I saw. Kodopolous was dead."

Madison glanced at Kelvey. "I didn't see a murder gun."

Kelvey's gaze pinned Ruggles. "It's his story. Let him tell it."

"I didn't touch a thing," said Ruggles. "The smell of gunpowder made me cough. I took a few steps inside and saw the body. For a few seconds I couldn't believe what I was seeing. I almost tossed my cookies, but then I got a grip and ran out and alerted Security. All so this cop could look at me like he don't believe a word I'm saying."

Kelvey said, "Someone backstage killed Kodopolous. The door was locked from the inside. There are no windows in that dressing room. You tell me, Ruggles. What did happen to the murder gun? What happened to the killer?"

"Aw, who do we think we're kidding?" Ruggles made an angry gesture. "We know who killed the guy. It was those damn cult crazies you hooked up with, Tony. George saw one of them back here looking for you or something and it got him killed."

Jardeen and Carolyn Gentry sent sharp glances of displeasure at Ruggles.

Three years earlier Jardeen had joined a trendy New Age

cult and had become a disciple of its charismatic matriarchal leader, Selma Balbor. He'd signed over most of his worldly possessions to the Order of World Harmony and went to live for a year in the Order's commune in the jungles of South America. He used his next CD to become the most prominent spokesperson of Balbor's teachings, which embraced a variety of eccentric notions from the channeling of dead spirits to cosmology, the notion that mankind was an experiment undertaken by extraterrestrials; far out stuff by any measure, and yet Selma Balbor's controversial books, tapes, DVD's and personal appearances had generated a following that numbered in the hundreds of thousands worldwide.

Jardeen said, "Larry, we went over this with the Lieutenant. If it had been the Order, they would have stayed to finish the job and killed me. Those people are automatons when they're on a mission."

Madison tugged at an earlobe.

"So the Order of World Harmony is sending out hit men? I guess that's one way to achieve world harmony. Kill anyone who doesn't agree with you."

Jardeen began to softly strum his guitar, lowering his eyes to watch his fingers on the frets. "Uh, there is a rumor that there's a contract out on me. Not from Selma but, well, there is a militant faction in the Order. I saw it once I was on the inside. I heard whispers. Beatings. People who had dropped out being harassed and threatened. That's one of the reasons I quit. But I'm sure that this talk about her people being out to kill me is, well, just crazy."

Ruggles sneered. "You mean crazy like Jonestown, or Charlie Manson–type crazy? These things do happen, man."

Madison wondered how Carolyn Gentry was reacting to this, but he kept his eyes on Jardeen.

"I read that you and Selma Balbor were romantically involved."

"No comment."

"I read that your new CD is an attack on her."

Jardeen stopped strumming and looked up as if trying to make up his mind.

"Okay, I know you're here to help. Here's how it is between me and the Order. I immersed myself in the life denial-of-worldly-possessions that Selma preaches, but I ultimately came to realize that I was only escaping reality, not coping with it. All of these gurus with their instant cures for society and people's troubles are really offering only one sure thing: get in touch with yourself. Tap what's already in you and put that to work. You can get that from a two-dollar secondhand book or a therapist . . . or you can hook up with an outfit like the Order of World Harmony and get suckered out of everything you've worked for and become and end up in a brainwashed commune down in the jungle where they'll tell you the same thing. That's what my new songs are about. That's what the new CD and this tour are all about. In addition to earning a few bucks, of course.

"Most of the people I met in the Order were well-meaning everyday folks looking for spiritual enlightenment like most of the New Age movement; people who hope the new millennium will lead to a higher level of collective awareness. But the problem with most of these gurus and their theories, channeling and the like, is that it's one-hundred-percent speculation. I do believe that there's more to reality than what we can see or touch, but now I'm skeptical of anyone who lines their pockets while purveying some spiritual Truth."

Madison said, "I'm waiting for you to say something I don't agree with."

Jardeen chuckled. "I'll stick with the facts. Three years ago the Order of World Harmony had half a million members, worldwide. But times are changing. Membership has dropped way off. People are wising up. Selma Balbor hates what I'm saying because it reflects on her and her organization. I'm costing her millions in revenue. But for her to send hit men after me, I just don't know."

There was a knock at the door.

Shapiro went to see who it was. Two deputies stood there. They wanted to speak with Kelvey. Kelvey exited the dressing room with some show of reluctance, closing the door after him.

Ruggles glared at the closed door and muttered an obscenity.

Shapiro glanced at his watch. "Showtime, Tony. Might be less heat for you out there than back here."

Jardeen nodded and rose, gripping the guitar casually by its neck. He clasped Carolyn Gentry's hand and drew a deep breath, exhaling quickly like a basketball player about to make a crucial shot.

"Come on, gang, let's get to it."

Shapiro acted as doorman for Tony and Carolyn. No one seemed to notice that the round of introductions had not included Carolyn, who hadn't said a word. Shapiro trailed out after them.

Madison and Ruggles started to follow when Kelvey and his two uniformed officers filled the doorway, each of whom had a hand resting on a holstered sidearm.

Kelvey toted a black leather traveling bag.

Ruggles' eyes widened. "Hey, what's the idea? That's mine."

"That's just what I was going ask." Kelvey faced Ruggles and held the bag between them open for inspection.

"Maybe you can identify what my men found inside."

Madison stepped closer to look at what Ruggles saw.

A snub-nosed revolver was snuggled in amid socks and a jogging suit.

Ruggles eyes bulged. "I never saw that gun before in my life. I don't even own a gun."

Kelvey shifted the bag to one hand and with the other he grabbed Ruggles by the arm and pushed him none too gently at the officers who seized Ruggles by either arm.

Madison cleared his throat. "Uh, how do you know that's the murder gun?"

Kelvey said. "We don't . . . yet. But you figure it. That gun has been fired recently, once. I think ballistics will match it with the bullet that killed George Kodopolous." He said to his men, "Boys, seal him off and read him his rights."

Ruggles was sullen and silent as they led him away. Madison and Kelvey stepped into the corridor.

Jardeen and his band were running from the wings onto the Red Rocks stage, the backing musicians scurrying to their instruments while Tony stepped into a circle of spotlight at center stage. The cheering swept down upon him from the immense crowd like a breaking wave.

Carolyn stood in the wings, watching, her back to Madison, unaware of what had just occurred.

Shapiro stood next to her. He shifted his gaze just in time to see Ruggles and his police escort disappear around a corner. Shapiro said nothing to Carolyn but left her side and strode over to Madison and Kelvey.

"What the hell's going on? Larry couldn't have done it! He's got some bluster to him but he's no killer."

Kelvey said, "It looks like he kicked that door in and shot Kodopolous, then stashed his gun and went looking for

Security. It's open and shut except for a confession."

"And a motive," said Madison. "It's too neat, Lieutenant, your boys finding that gun. Ruggles is being set up. Can't you smell it?"

"I'm getting paid to think my way, not think yours," said Kelvey. "Don't worry about Ruggles. It happens this way a lot of times. Most homicides are wrapped up within an hour of the murder. I'll question him so he knows he's been questioned, but that's all I'm going to do for now. No one leaves this crime scene except for that and his band while they're onstage."

"Understood," said Shapiro.

Kelvey stalked off down the corridor.

Onstage, Tony Jardeen and his band kicked off with a hard-rocking version of *Storm the Walls*, one of Madison's favorites from Tony's first CD.

Shapiro regarded Madison with profound dismay. "Steve, we've got to do something. Maybe Kelvey's right. Maybe Ruggles did kill Kodopolous. But I know Larry Ruggles. He and Tony and Kodopolous have been a unit since Tony's career began. I can't believe Larry would do this."

"Is that anything more than a hunch?"

"Well, no." Shapiro stuck out his chin. "But since you're here and since I am picking up the tab, I want you to nose around some more. Play it however you like, the way you always do. But let's see what you dig up. I can help. I've got enough yes people here to run what's left of the show. What do you want me to do?"

"Okay," said Madison. "Find out where they took Ruggles. When Kelvey comes out, find out what he's learned. Stay on top of that angle."

"Will do. You'll hear from me the minute anything breaks."

Shapiro walked away briskly.

Madison paused, part of him wishing that he could avoid what he had to do next.

He ambled up the ramp to where Carolyn stood, beyond sight of the bobbing tiers of paying customers. He had an up-close view of everything happening onstage, and of a grassy stretch of ground directly below the stage, separating the stage from a mesh fence and the first rows of the audience beyond.

The grassy patch was patrolled by five burly security men, their rippling muscles encased in Tony Jardeen T-shirts. They stood evenly distanced from each other, their backs to the stage, hands clasped before them, facing the audience.

Onstage, Tony launched into another number, *Spirits Need to Shake.*

Carolyn's attention shifted to Madison.

"Hello, Carolyn."

"Steve." She said it like the start of a sentence that she could not finish. Her voice was warm and throaty as he remembered it, even raised slightly for him to hear her through the sound and fury of the band. She said, "How have you been, Stephen? It was . . . sort of a surprise seeing you here today." Her eyes were troubled with feeling.

Madison had just gone into business for himself as a music industry troubleshooter and she'd been a stringer for *Rolling Stone* when they fell in love. Her eyes told him, *I'm another man's woman now,* and that she intended to hold her emotions in check.

He said, "Carolyn, I'm here to do a job."

"Larry Ruggles didn't kill George Kodopolous."

"That's what Arn says. Any idea who did?"

She pointed. "See that security guard over by the far end of the stage? I—I think he could be part of some plot to get

Tony. I think Larry's right about that Balbor witch being behind what happened to George Kodopolous. Or maybe I'm just paranoid."

She was indicating a blond-haired, hefty young man who was barely distinguishable from the four other security men on the grass below.

"Why you do suspect him?"

"Well, he's not doing it now, but during the first two songs he seemed more interested in looking over his shoulder at Tony than in keeping his attention on the audience like he's supposed to, as if he was positioning Tony in his mind for something."

"I'll keep my eye on him."

She nodded and said nothing more, her concentration returning to the show.

Tony had slowed the tempo and was singing his current hit, the mid-tempo *Livin' for Free*.

Madison watched the blond-haired security man, but while under his scrutiny, the guy did not once turn to look over his shoulder at Tony. He did his job expertly when over-zealous fans breached the fence and tried to rush the stage, the security team working together like a drill team to hustle the intruders off the grassy area before resuming their positions for the next onslaught.

Madison thought, *Maybe Carolyn is wrong.*

Jardeen was singing and playing his way into a well-paced set. The fans loved it. The chant-like *World Harmony Blues*, a thinly veiled, scathing indictment of Selma Balbor, garnered an enthusiastic response.

Madison noticed that Carolyn's attention never wavered from the star.

"Is it as serious as it looks with you and Tony?" he asked during a lull in the show while Jardeen was introducing the members of his band.

"He wants to marry me," she said without meeting his gaze, "and I want him to marry me."

"He's made a good choice," said Madison. "He's getting a fine woman for a wife. I'm sorry it didn't work out between us, hon. I really am."

She said, "But that was yesterday, and we're living in the present, right?"

He thought he heard a twinge of doubt in her voice.

"Right," he said, not unkindly. "Does Tony know about us?"

"Past loves are something we don't talk about by mutual consent. I drifted after you and I broke up, Steve. You broke my heart big time. I got into some pretty weird, dead-end scenes for awhile there. Then I met Tony. He's a sweet and caring man, Steve, and he's in love with me. I'm taking another chance on love."

"Then I hope it works for you, Carolyn. You deserve that after the way I treated you."

"You could have behaved better," she said, "but I've forgiven you. We put each other through a lot. If it had been right, it would have worked."

"What about today? Did you know Kodopolous?"

"I only met him today." Her eyes followed the man onstage. "George Kodopolous was an infamous letch, I've heard that about him. Maybe that caught up with him."

"Where were you when he was killed?"

She regarded him again, more coolly than before. "Am I a murder suspect?"

"I told you, Carolyn. I'm on a job. Kelvey must have asked you that question. What did you tell him?"

She sighed. "I was in Tony's dressing room, where you saw me. I was alone. I heard the shot and at first I didn't realize what it was. Tony was with his musicians. I don't suppose that gives me much of an alibi, but then I didn't think I'd need one. I didn't know a man was going to be killed."

Tony and his band kicked off another rocker.

Madison let the conversation slide. He tried to ignore emotions of regret he felt stirring within him.

There was no sign of Shapiro, Kelvey or Ruggles.

The security man Carolyn had pointed out continued to appear wholly occupied with taking care of business, with crowd control and nothing else. Madison watched him anyway.

Tony's band was in full flight. The crowd was going wild. Everyone was on their feet, cheering thunderously and singing along.

After a few more songs, the blond-haired security man turned abruptly, drawing a gun that had been tucked into his waist beneath the T-shirt. A snub-nose .38 extended from his right fist, the arm ascending in a rapid arc, tracking on Tony in front of the wailing band less than twenty feet away. The other security men on the grassy area had so much else demanding their attention—the pandemonium of fans crushing against the mesh fence—that they were unaware of what was occurring within their own ranks.

Madison sprinted from the wings, dashing across the stage past Jardeen and the band. Someone realized what was happening and a scream pierced the roar of music and audience. Madison left the stage in a dive that sent him flying into the gunman just as the guy got his sights on Tony. Air whoofed out of the man's lungs, his gun arm tilted skyward.

The impact of the collision sent them both tumbling, the pistol discharging close to Madison's left ear. They sprawled across the ground, Madison on top. The downed man snarled, attempting to throw Madison off. Madison's right fist closed around the guy's gun hand, jerking it back hard and fast. Wrist bones snapped. The guy howled and released the gun. Madison grabbed the .38 and whapped it crossways, a strong backhand. The butt of the gun caught the young man smartly across his right temple. His eyes rolled back in his head until only the whites showed and the back of his head flopped against the grassy turf. He was unconscious like a berserk robot with its juice suddenly cut.

Madison got to his feet, unholstering the .44 in case blondie had accomplices. Apparently, there were none. He turned toward the stage to see if the fired shot had done any damage. His ears were ringing.

The band's playing had dissipated to a ragged halt but everyone up there, including Tony, appeared safe enough. Uniformed police and security personnel were charging out from backstage. Carolyn emerged from the wings, hurrying to Tony's side. They were both in a mild state of shock like everyone else around them. Tony put his arms around her. The crowd was still thundering at full-throttle, not grasping what had just occurred, it had happened so fast.

The would-be assassin was recovering consciousness as the police swooped in, handcuffed him and brusquely hauled him away.

Onstage, Tony and Carolyn parted with a kiss. Carolyn returned to the wings. Sensing that things were under control and that most of his audience had not even heard the shot, Tony launched back into the song they'd been playing. He looked sideways and caught Madison's eye with a nod that seemed to say, *Thanks, man! I'll talk to you after the show.*

Kelvey reappeared with Shapiro at his side. There was

no sign of Larry Ruggles. The music prohibited Madison from overhearing, but it was apparent that Kelvey was advising the prisoner of his rights, that he was under arrest. Blondie was led down the ramp by Kelvey and the others, into the corridor and taken away in the same direction as Ruggles had been taken. Kelvey was too busy to confer with Madison. His people had apparently filled him in on Madison's role in what had just occurred. But Madison knew cops well enough to know that before this day was over he would be relating his story many times for the record. Then there was the media.

When the backstage excitement had dissipated somewhat, he managed to catch Carolyn's attention and indicated a nonverbal invitation to join him in a relatively quiet corner where Arn Shapiro was just finishing a call on his cell phone. Carolyn nodded and advanced to join them.

Something was percolating in Madison's brain just below the surface of conscious thought, but he could not put his finger on it. He was too busy fending off *"Are you okay"* and *"Good job"* from assorted backstagers.

He reached the corner at the same time as Carolyn, who said, "Thank you, Steve. That was a very heroic thing you did."

Shapiro nodded without enthusiasm. "Yeah, he does good work. That's why I pay him the big bucks."

Madison said to Arn, "So what did Kelvey get from the security guy?"

"Not much and I couldn't hear very well with everything that was going on," said Arn. "I didn't catch his name if he gave it. All I heard him say was that he was an instrument of Selma Balbor's will. End quote." Shapiro pocketed his cell phone. "I was just talking to my head of security. The guy wrangled a job for this show and I intend to find out how."

"What about Ruggles?"

"Haven't heard a thing. Kelvey still has him under wraps. He ought to be released after what just happened. That security man killed Kodopolous just like Ruggles said."

Madison tugged at his earlobe. "Maybe it happened that way. Arn, you go on hanging close to Kelvey."

"Glad to. And, Steve . . ." Shapiro seemed to have trouble finding words. "Uh, you did one hell of a job out there."

He withdrew, leaving Madison alone with Carolyn.

She regarded him with concern. "What did he say about Larry? The police don't suspect him of killing Kodopolous, do they?"

"They have reason enough," said Madison. "Isn't that what you wanted everyone to think when you planted the murder gun in Ruggles' bag?"

His percolating thought had surfaced.

She drew back. "What are you saying?"

"You know what I'm saying, Carolyn. You shot and killed George Kodopolous."

She raised a hand to her throat. Her eyes were like saucers. She hesitated before replying.

"I can't believe you'd say that."

"I hope I'm wrong but I don't think I am. I'll tell Kelvey what I think; then it's in his hands."

"Steve, wait. Can we go somewhere quiet and talk?"

A surge of anger coursed through him. "Why? So you can blow out my brains too? Isn't one a day enough for you?"

She touched his arm; her fingers were like talons. "I can explain."

Onstage, Tony and his band eased into a down-tempo

song played in a minor key. Voice and instruments moaned low.

"If it happened the way I think it did," said Madison, "you could get away with it. You and Tony both told me what a letch Kodopolous was. What did he do, Carolyn? What was his sin? Did he try to get you into his bed?"

He saw her spirit break then, as quickly as it took him to speak those words. Something within her died.

"Not his bed. He wanted to . . . do it right there in his goddamn dressing room with Tony down the hall getting ready for the concert. Steve, it was terrible."

"I think I know what happened," he said. "I think you've met Kodopolous before; you being Tony's girlfriend and him being Tony's agent, it would be hard for you not to meet. I think he'd been on the letch for you for awhile and he thought he had a way to get you to put out. He started threatening you with blackmail and it all came to a head here today. Somehow he found out that you'd been a member of the Order of World Harmony. He threatened to tell Tony."

She blinked. "How do you know that?"

"I've been thinking about it. That security guy who tried to shoot Tony, he was a member of Selma Balbor's organization. Tony didn't recognize him because the guy made sure to face away from the stage like a good security man should. You did recognize him from where you were standing in the wings and you told me to keep an eye on him . . . *before he did anything suspicious.* You made up that story about him watching Tony over his shoulder. You had a good idea why he was here. You couldn't tell me the truth, about recognizing him because you'd been a cult member, so you made up the story about him acting suspicious. If it had been that way, he would've looked over his shoulder at least one time while I was watching him. Layman psychology maybe, but it makes sense to me. The guy didn't turn around once while I was watching until it was time to open fire. He had the whole scenario worked out like clockwork before he did it. It was lucky that I was watching him. Well, not lucky. You *told* me to watch him. You saved Tony's life as much as I did. And since the guy didn't make any moves before the attempt, the only one way you could have recognized him is if you were a member of Selma Balbor's cult."

She cast her eyes downward.

"I belonged to that crazy woman's cult for a whole six weeks. I told you that I went through some changes after we broke up. The Order was one of them. You're right, Steve. That's where I recognized him from."

"As for Kodopolous," said Madison, "the killer had to be someone backstage, and this is a highly restricted area. Tony didn't kill Kodopolous. He was with his band when the murder was committed. Shapiro isn't a suspect. He and Kodopolous made big money for each other and Arn would never do anything that would stop him from making a profit. Larry Ruggles? The frame was too good. Even Kelvey wasn't sure if he should buy it. That left you."

"I don't know how Kodopolous found out but he did and yes, he made his threat this afternoon, the smarmy pig. It would have meant the end of everything for me if he'd gone to Tony with it."

"Why didn't you tell Tony?"

"I was afraid to. Tony puts honesty above everything and I have been honest with him about everything . . . except that. My life looks perfect with Tony, I didn't want it to fall apart the way it did for you and me."

She spewed out the rest as if relieved to purge herself of the secret she'd been carrying. If Kodopolous told Tony,

Tony would have forever doubted his fiancée, never sure if Carolyn wasn't a plant by Selma Balbor. He would never forgive her for not having leveled with him about her past. When Kodopolous made his threats and put his hands on her, Carolyn knew that if she allowed it, he'd use his knowledge over her whenever he felt in the mood. And so she killed him.

Madison heard her out, then said, "The part I don't get is when Ruggles found him, the door was locked from the inside."

Her gaze had never lifted from a downward cast.

"Larry was pounding on the door right after it happened." Her words came deliberately now in the flat monotone of resignation. "I stepped against the wall next to the door when Larry forced his way in."

"He really didn't see you, or is he covering for you?"

"He didn't see me. I hid behind the door when he kicked it open. He came into the room and stood there in shock, looking down at the body like he said, and while he was doing that, I slipped out behind him."

The confession tapered off after that. She knew she was wrong to plant the gun in Ruggles' bag but if there was any real danger of his being convicted for the crime, she would come forward and confess. She raised her gaze to meet his, and her eyes were full of pain and sadness.

"My God, Steve. Oh, my God."

"I'm sorry, honey. I'm going to find Kelvey."

"Honey. So it's going to fall apart with Tony. After the terrible thing I've done, I guess it's what I deserve. I know that. But . . ." Her eyes matched the pleading in her voice. "What if you kept this just between the two of us? Larry will be okay or I'll come forward, I swear. But if this blows over the way I think it will . . . couldn't we just try it? I was defending myself. Dammit, Steve, that pervert should have kept his hands off me. With Tony I have finally found everything I've always wanted. Don't ruin it for me *again*."

"Stop it," he said. "This has nothing to do with what happened between us before. You will take responsibility for snuffing out that man's life, Carolyn, no matter how much he deserved it. I'm not going to allow Ruggles to have his name tarnished for life with the suspicion of murder hanging over his head just because he was in the wrong place at the wrong time. I won't do that."

She drew back. Her eyes tightened, as did the line of her mouth.

"You're a bastard."

"And you're a murderess. But I don't have any proof of that. Maybe you can stay solid with Tony if you come clean, I don't know. I'm sorry. I really am."

Her features softened. "You always were the most honest bastard I ever knew." She placed her forehead against the wall and began to cry.

Madison walked away.

Tony and the band had picked up the tempo again with a hard-edged rocker.

Carolyn cried out, "Steve . . . *please!*" But she did not come after him.

And he could not look back.

THE DEATH BLUES

Saddle up my pony,
Hitch up my brown mare.
You know my baby's
Out in the world somewhere . . .

Carl Hensman looked up at me excitedly from the old 78-rpm record spinning on the turntable. He was a wiry, studious looking guy with thinning blond hair, in his mid-thirties.

"No one's ever been able to sing like that. It's a voice like no other. And all these years everyone thought he was dead."

"Let it play," I said.

The pure blues voice was low and sorrowful, but strong enough to ride over the crackling, popping surface noise that buried most of the backing combo.

When the record was over, Hensman lifted the tone arm gingerly. He flicked off the stereo and looked back at me, waiting for a reaction. We'd met in a jazz bar two years earlier and had been getting together to play records about once a week ever since. It was a Saturday night and this week we were at his place.

When I still didn't say anything, he said, "You know how I klutz these things up. A real social magician. I love their music but I'll be damned if I can relate to the people. The place was closed for business but I did talk to the owner. He couldn't or wouldn't tell me a thing. He denied even knowing a Stomper Crawford."

"But, Carl, how can you be so *sure* it was Crawford?"

"I'm not sure," he admitted, some of the excitement returning. "But isn't it worth a follow-up? You're a private detective, O'Dair. Stuff like this is your business. And think of what it could mean if it was him—if you do track him down. I've been sitting on that money for three years waiting for the right artist to come along. So I look out of a bus window and who do I see stepping into a bar? Damn! If I could record Stomper Crawford, it would be the blues rediscovery of the century!"

"Or decade. But it was a moving bus, Carl. Stomper Crawford hasn't recorded since nineteen fifty-nine. It's been longer than that since his last publicity picture. He could look like a different person by now."

"So then I'm wrong and all we have are our records. Just what we started with. Nothing more, nothing less."

There was no way I could argue that one. There was no way I wanted to. I told him so, and that I might as well get right on it. The bars uptown would be in full swing. That might make things easier.

"Be sure to call me as soon as you learn anything," he mother-henned on the way to the door. "Don't worry about the hour. And tell him we'll record him with any sidemen he likes. Any type of material he likes, too. I'd like to recut some of the old stuff, but it would be terrific if we had some new songs, too."

"What was the name of that bar?"

"*Leon's.* On Thirty-fourth. I wasn't but four minutes behind him but he couldn't be found."

"Okay," I said. "I'm on my way. I'll check the place out."

"And remember, O'Dair. Don't forget to call me when you've found him. No matter what the hour."

"I'll remember, Carl."

★ ★ ★ ★ ★

Leon's on Thirty-fourth was in the heart of the city's black section.

I'd worked these neighborhoods in the hungry days when bail bondsmen had been my clients and when someone had jumped, it was my job to bring them in. I knew my way around, and I still had friends.

Leon Miller had saved my life once and we had stayed in touch. His round black face lit up when I took a seat at his bar.

"O'Dair, my man! Long time no see, brother. I was beginning to think you was either dead or married!"

"Just busy, Leon. How've you been?"

We kicked around the conversational ball for awhile. The place was busy with a Saturday night crowd and the walls, hidden somewhere beyond the swirling haze of cigarette smoke, throbbed to the pulsating disco from the jukebox and the constant din of raised voices. It took awhile for me to get around to why I was there. Finally, there was a break in the action and we got some time to sit at the end of the bar over a couple of beers.

"A guy came in here this afternoon," I said. "A white guy. He was looking for Stomper Crawford."

Leon's face clouded in the dimness.

"Stomp Crawford? Now that goes back, man. Stomp was one of the big ones in the old days before he dropped out of sight."

"This white guy looks like Woody Allen. Acts like him too. Says he's sure he saw Stomper coming in here this afternoon about five. He talked to someone. I guess that was you."

"It was me." He grinned. "That boy looked like his mommy just dropped him off all alone on the wrong end of town. But I told him the truth, O'Dair. Stomper wasn't in here today. No way."

"He's pretty sure, Leon."

Leon's voice lowered to make a point. I had to lean forward to catch his words.

"I'm telling you like it is, O'Dair. Me and Stomp Crawford go way back together, man. He used to play here all the time. I'm married to his cousin. Wouldn't be anyone gladder to see Stomper than me. But Stomper Crawford disappeared eight years ago and ain't been heard from since. Left his band, his family, everyone else high and dry, and that's a natural fact."

"Okay, Leon. Thanks. If he ever does walk in the door, give me a call, okay?"

"You'll be the first to know, baby. The first to know."

We shook on it and I edged my way out of the club. People parted slowly. There were one or two "Excuse me's." But no smiles.

Outside, the pavement still radiated the heat of summer's sun even though it was well past eleven p.m. The street was alive. Bright colors and the latest fashions paraded by to the music of powerful gunning exhausts and the calls of young men to the ladies.

I moved up the sidewalk and around the corner to where I'd parked my car a half block down on a cross street. The nighttime symphony at my back receded with each step until the darkness around me was almost silent again.

I was fitting my key into the car door lock when I heard the scuffling of feet as they rushed me from behind, from the opposite curb. I started to turn but they were on me by then. A savage kick from the side knocked my ankles out from below. When I came up a moment later I was being pulled and held by a dude from behind while the guy in front went to work.

He must have done time in the ring when he wasn't beating people up on the street. Black, dressed in black, he was a blur in the night as he danced before me, stiff-arming left and right killer punches that popped me like hammer blows.

"We don't like competition, honky," snarled the one in front as a right from way back made my knees buckle. Things started swimming in my field of vision. "Go home, and don't come back. Forget Stomper Crawford, dig?"

The one holding me stepped back and I slumped. The whole thing had taken less than thirty seconds and hardly made any noise. I hit the pavement like a kid's forgotten marionette. Only I wasn't forgotten. I knew what would come next. These guys wanted to put me out of commission.

I gazed along at the level of the sidewalk. I saw the toe of the fighter's right shoe pull back for the kick that would end the job. But there wasn't a damn thing I could do about it. The professional beating had left me paralyzed with pain. I'd be able to move in a minute or two, but a lot of good that would do me now.

Then there was someone with us. A third someone who came thundering down the street at us from the direction of the club.

"Hey, what's going on?" a voice shouted.

The foot rested. The fighter held his ground.

"Beat it, brother. This is a private argument."

But the curious voice kept coming and in another instant there was a full-scale brawl going on over my head, and these guys weren't playing. I heard a fist sink into someone's gut and push the wind out. A body slammed back into a car, my car. Another punch into another body. Again. Someone grunted in pain. Someone swore. Then two pairs of feet slapping away on the pavement, disappearing into the night.

Things were starting to fade back into focus but the pain was still there, and it would get worse. I knew that from experience.

The guy helping me to my feet wasn't much into his twenties, if that. He was good looking, lithe, with that muscular wiriness a black man needs to survive in the ghetto.

"You all right, man?"

I leaned back against the car.

"Yeah, I'm all right, or most of me is. Thanks. That's one I owe you."

"That's okay. You got me curious back there in the club so I followed you out. I heard you were looking for Stomper Crawford."

"You heard right. Can you help me find him?"

"Maybe. My name is Isaac Crawford. Stomper's my old man."

Stomper had gained about forty pounds and had gone through a lot of pain since his heyday in the early 1950s. I remember the old publicity photos I'd seen reproduced in the blues history books. Stomper Crawford had been young, wild, hungry, eager to please. His eyes and smile had flashed with the knowledge that he was Number One on the charts of what was then called "race records."

Now he was tired. He sat on the sagging couch in the apartment living room. The old two-strap undershirt rode down over the bulge of his stomach, its whiteness in stark contrast to the ebony of his skin. He wore an expression of weary resignation.

"A man just can't stay on the run forever. Eight years was long enough, traveling from town to town, working odd jobs." He glanced in the direction of his son, who sat beside him. "I've got my roots here. And my son Isaac didn't think poorly of me for having ducked trouble all that time."

Side by side, you knew they were father and son. Isaac could have doubled for those old publicity shots. Young, wild, hungry. But not so eager to please.

"Thing is, we don't need an outsider messing things up," he told me pointedly. His stare was a blunt as his words.

The aches from the roughhousing back on the street were all but forgotten now. I was still trying to believe that finding Crawford had been this easy. But it's like that sometimes. It was like that now.

I looked at Crawford senior. Surviving the hard times had given him the kind of silent dignity you often find in black men of his age. He wasn't the type of guy you spoke around as if he weren't there.

"I don't understand how you think I could gum things up," I said. "If anything, I've confirmed for you what were only suspicions before. You came back not knowing if there'd be people after you. I drew them out. Now you know. That should count for something."

"It does," agreed the old man. "That's why Isaac brought you here to see me. Now you understand. Now you can go back and tell your producer friend and he'll understand, too. Right now I've got all the help I'll need, Mr. O'Dair. Isaac's a good son. He'll see me through. Maybe then we can talk business. I'd like to talk business now but—"

He ended with an expressive shrug. He appreciated my

coming by, my offer of assistance, but blood was thicker.

I looked at Isaac.

"How do you intend to help your father?"

"My group has this block and the ten square blocks around it." The response was heavy with a young man's macho pride. "Dad's going to start his comeback by playing the local clubs again. Leon's already said he could play at his place."

"Is that what you were doing there this afternoon?" I asked Stomper. "Lining up a gig?"

Stomper nodded.

"Leon was surprised as hell to see me after all these years," he chuckled. "I told him keep it under his hat until I got things squared away. I guess he did."

Right, I thought. Leon was married to Stomper's cousin. Blood was always thicker. So is race. At least it had been between Leon and me.

I glanced back at Isaac. There was nothing even resembling trust in his eyes but he was keeping it inside in deference to his parent.

"Is it safe to expose your father like that?" I asked. "Those two guys tonight were pros. They could get luckier when it comes to your old man. There could be more of them."

The angry face tightened.

"Let those dudes try for my father in my own territory. They're welcome to what we lay on them."

Stomper read my expression.

"Don't get the idea my Isaac's in some neighborhood gang," he justified. "It's a Neighborhood Action Group, they call it. There's a whole world of difference. They've done plenty for this neighborhood: food relief, a day care center for kids whose folks have got to work, helping out teenagers on dope. They're the new generation. They've got new ideas and the energy to back them up."

"No one's questioning their motives," I said. "But wasting whoever comes around to waste you is the wrong way to work it. Think of it. Your comeback and that violence will go hand-in-hand. Something like that always follows you, Stomper."

"We take care of our own on this end of town," Isaac bristled defiantly.

"It's something that could always be dug up and used against you," I pressed at the old man. "What this guy Hensman is offering you is a legitimate comeback. A ticket back into the recording studio. You've already got the name back from the old days. Your seventy-eights are reissued all the time. People are starved for something new by Stomper Crawford. Let Hensman produce a session. He'll put up the money, but it'll be your show. He'll market the tapes to a label and you're in business again."

Isaac had heard enough.

"Yeah, right out where some sucker can nail him. I say we start small. Isolate whoever it is. Nail THEM! Then Dad will be free to do whatever he wants without having to look over his shoulder all his life. But we've got to do it here in the neighborhood where I can keep things covered. We're strong here. Out there we're vulnerable."

"By 'out there,' you mean out of the ghetto. The ghetto is where the trouble started, remember, Isaac?" I looked back at Stomper. "Run it by me one more time," I suggested. "Maybe Isaac and I can both help."

"Maybe you can at that," the old man nodded. "But I don't see what good going over it again would do. You think I haven't been over it enough during the last eight years to last me a lifetime? But it was dark. I didn't see a thing and that's God's truth. I just wish these bad dudes would believe me." His eyes got a faraway look. "I was the King of the Blues, that's what they called me. Then rock & roll came in and the young kids who bought the records didn't want to hear us old-timers anymore. But if I wasn't a star, I could still draw them in my own neighborhood. Yes sir, in the bars around here they *knew* how good my band was! Yes, indeed. But then some joker with a fast knife had to take that away from me, too."

"You saw a man get wasted in the alley out back of *Leon's* while you were taking a break," I said. "Didn't Leon ever get curious and try to follow it up?"

"Follow what up?" he sighed. "Whoever did it split when they saw my shadow but they must have hung around. I went over and saw that the dude they'd left behind was dead—his throat was cut ear to ear—and I went back inside to get Leon. By the time I found him and we got back out there again, the stiff was gone. Those boys knew their business. Two held him and the third did the cutting, and they cleaned up after themselves real neat and tidy when they were done. Wasn't a damn thing to call the cops about!"

"Not that they didn't give a damn," growled Isaac. "It's a tough couple of blocks down there after dark. Hookers, pimps, pushers, guys on junk. A lot of heavy stuff goes down. It could have been anything, what Dad saw. The cops don't like to come up to this end of town unless they have to."

"Somebody thought you saw some faces," I reminded Stomper, as if he needed reminding. "The cops could have helped on that."

Stomper treated the remark as being too foolish—or too idealistic—to deserve a response.

"I should have kept my mouth shut," he said as if still

not sure why he hadn't. "But I told some of the cats on the bandstand before the next set started. Word gets around."

"So somebody started throwing bullets at you the next day and after two near misses you decided it was time to split town. Now it's eight years later and you're back—and you're right back where you were before you left if you go back to haunting the old neighborhood and playing the same old bars. I'm offering you a way out of that, Stomper."

"My father is through running, O'Dair." That was Isaac. The growl had become a snarl. He turned to his father, his voice heavy with emotion. "Dad, send this dude back downtown where he belongs. He'll bring you nothing but trouble. Let me handle this thing for you like we agreed. You know I can do it."

"I know you can, son," said the old man slowly. "But you've got to admit there's some sense to what Mr. O'Dair says, too. If we're vulnerable outside the ghetto, so are the boys who are after me. You did say you were a private detective, Mr. O'Dair?"

"I did and I am. Consider me your bodyguard, if you want me. Call it a payment for all the good times I've had listening to your records. Every time I played one, I'd wonder what happened to you. Now that we've found you, I'll keep you healthy. If something did happen to you now and Isaac didn't do me in, Carl Hensman probably would. That's a lot of incentive to keep you breathing."

The younger Crawford was suddenly on his feet. He knew which way the conversation was heading and he didn't like it. His hands were clenched and you could almost feel the heat of his anger.

"Ever since Mama died it's been just me and you," he snarled at his father. "All the time you were gone, whenever you wrote me, I always kept quiet about where you were, just like you said. You came back and I've kept quiet about that, too. All to help you. So now you throw in with the first honky dude off the street who walks in with a smooth line. How do you know he isn't one of them? Haven't you been ripped off enough by every white man you ever signed a recording contract with? Isn't that enough for you? Your record sales bought them Cadillacs while your own family had to wear rags. But you still fall for the same jive!"

Now it was Crawford senior's turn to growl.

"That'll be enough talk like that, Isaac. I respect Mr. O'Dair as an honest man and there's truth to what he's saying. I don't see why the three of us can't work together on this."

"Because I don't work with the enemy," Isaac told him. Then he turned both the snarl and the glare towards me. "If anything happens to my father, I'm laying it on your shoulders, man. I'll find you and kill you with my bare hands."

Then he spun on his heel and was gone, the door slamming behind him, the heat of his anger seeming to remain, a brittle, almost tangible thing in the sudden stillness of the room.

Stomper Crawford gazed at the front door which his son had slammed. He seemed even more tired than before and when he spoke it was if he were reciting the lyrics to some new blues song.

"Damn! It looks like I'm gaining a career and losing a son. Damn . . ."

Stomper wouldn't leave the apartment that night. He told me that it was Isaac's place. He wanted to wait until Isaac came back. They had to have a talk. So I called Hensman from there and told him the news. It sounded for

226

a while there like he was going to have a cardiac arrest. Then I put Stomper on and they talked for nearly a half-hour.

Stomper told Carl only that he had "personal problems" and that he wouldn't be able to get together until to-morrow, Sunday. Carl finally bought that and they agreed to meet at his, Carl's, place tomorrow morning at eleven. Bright and early, for a Sunday.

I stayed with Stomper that night, sitting up with him in his son's living room, sharing a bottle of whisky and lis-tening to tales—some of them tall, I imagine—about the good old days of the fifties when Stomper and his rollicking band had made blues history both in the recording studios and on a series of high-living around-the-year tours on the road.

I drifted off about three, still listening to him reminisce, both of us lazy and loose from the drinking, me feeling vaguely pleased with myself for my part in rediscovering a blues legend . . .

Isaac didn't show up that night, and by the time Stomper and I departed for Carl's at a little past ten-thirty the next morning, you could see that it was weighing heavily on the old man's mind. He had aged years during the night. But then I probably wasn't looking too hot my-self. I felt like hell.

Stomper Crawford and Carl Hensman, worlds apart in lifestyle and upbringing, became best friends the moment they met, drawn together by a deep love of and commit-ment to the blues, as well as by the knowledge on Stomper's part that Carl not only *could* but *would* help. The two don't always go together. Not in the world of Stomper Crawfords.

Carl had to hear the whole story straight from Stomper's

lips and you could tell that the tale fascinated him. Stomper's story was, for sure, the stuff of blues legend. Living legend. Top of the rhythm and blues charts all during the fifties. Pushed out by rock and roll. Back to playing the neighborhood juke joints that had spawned him. Then even that taken away eight years ago when he witnessed a murder, what had seemed to be a very professional hit. Now he was back and things were happening to him again.

I figured Stomper was safe at Carl's for the time being. I had kept my eyes open and no one had followed us there. So when the two of them started talking business, forgetting that I was even around, I cut out for about an hour and spent my time nosing around uptown again.

Back to the ghetto.

Looking and asking . . .

I had a surprise waiting for me when I got back to Carl's. Carl and the bluesman were waiting at the curb and they wasted no time in climbing into the front seat with me.

"Where to, guys?"

There was a moment's hesitation. Then Carl spoke, and you could tell that he knew I wouldn't like it.

"Stomper wants to go down to *Leon's*," he said. "They're closed this afternoon but he's going to have a private jam with some of his old sidemen. They're meeting us down there. Leon's making the calls."

We stayed at the curb. I tried to keep the exasperation out of my voice.

"Wait a minute, Stomper. The whole rift with Isaac last night was over how I wanted to get you OUT of the ghetto."

He'd been staring out the front windshield. Now he turned to face me.

228

"You wait a minute," he said without rancor but firmly. "I'm the man making the comeback. I'm the man who's going to decide how it's done. I'm too old to make a fool out of myself in public, O'Dair. I'm with you on everything you said last night. But it won't mean a thing if the *feel* isn't there anymore. Understand?"

"I tried to talk him out of it," put in Carl, next to the door, but you could tell that he thought the idea was terrific.

"I've got to be sure I can still do it, man," said Stomper firmly. "And *Leon's* is the place to find out."

I knew when I was licked.

And so we were on our way back to the club. Back into the belly of the inner city.

It was a quiet drive. Carl sensed my disapproval, but he was still flushed with that peculiar excitement of which only a truly fanatical music lover is capable. Stomper was silent, somber, staring out through the windshield as if he were seeing, or worrying about, more than the mild Sunday traffic.

I had a few worries of my own. I understood Stomper's side of it; I only wished he'd understand mine. He had the natural apprehension any artist feels upon returning to an art he's left untouched for years. But I was worried about the fact that I was driving him back to the scene where all his troubles had begun. At least, the problems involving violence and sudden death.

I was also worried about the fact that I was unarmed. The .357 I sometimes carried was back in my apartment. I hadn't been wearing it when I'd showed up at Carl's last night for our record listening, and I hadn't slowed down since.

I felt very naked. But I tried not to think about that . . .

Leon's was three steps below street level. Thirty-fourth Street had a completely different feel from last night. Then it had throbbed with the excitement of a night scene. Now the mid-afternoon sun beat down. There was no traffic on the sidewalks and little on the street.

I pulled up at the curb and the three of us piled out and across the sidewalk and down the narrow cement steps. Stomper tried the door. It was locked. He pounded a meaty fist on the metal and we waited. I caught Carl's glance over the bluesman's shoulder. Carl gave me an excited wink. The door opened.

Leon's round face burst into pure joy when he spotted Stomper on his doorstep. They threw their arms around each other, two happy men, slapping wildly, oblivious to anyone watching.

"It's my main man and he's gonna do it again!" laughed Leon. "You're the first one here, man. The other cats are on their way. Fall in and have some drinks!"

"Sounds good to me, brother," said Stomper. "You know O'Dair and Carl Hensman?"

"Hell yeah, how're you doing, O'Dair?" The question came at me along with a wide, infectious grin. To Carl, he said, "Welcome back to the club, my man. Let's go down-stairs and get the party rolling!"

You'd never guess that he was a man faced with the evidence that he had lied to me last night or to Carl yesterday afternoon. But things were moving too smoothly to bring that up now. We moved into the low-ceilinged tavern. It had that ghostly quiet which all bars somehow acquire during off-hours. But Leon's chatter seemed to warm the place up as we seated ourselves around a table and Leon served a round of drinks. Beer for three of us, cola for Carl.

Then Leon surprised me by bringing up what I had avoided.

"Hope there aren't any bad feelings about me bending the truth a little when you fellas came around looking for Stomper," he opened.

"No hard feelings here, Leon," I told him. "I gave it some thought. I'd have done the same if Stomper had asked me."

"No hard feelings at all," added Carl. "I'm just glad we're making this thing happen. It's really a historical event!"

Carl talks like that sometimes.

"I just hope it does happen," said Stomper, half to himself. "I've been away from music for a long time, ya know."

"Hell, you'll sound fine," Leon assured him. "Hey, Stomp, old Lefty Dugan's one of the cats coming down today. Remember the time the three of us went to that party over on Forty-second—"

With that they were off on an animated tangent regarding what Stomper's old crowd was up to these days.

Carl and I let the two of them carry the conversation, Carl eagerly absorbing these insights into the black culture behind the music he loved, me just happy to see Stomper relaxing, losing his troubles in talk. The tenseness I had noticed since last night seemed to be fading. If only temporarily, his troubles with Isaac appeared to be forgotten.

They'd been at it for about fifteen minutes when we heard the front door creak open. All eyes turned expectantly toward the entranceway as two sets of feet scuffled down unseen steps.

I caught a side-glance of Stomper. He seemed truly alive for the first time since we'd met. A vein twitched at his neck, as if expectantly.

But the two guys who came through the archway into the club weren't musicians. Their black faces were frozen masks, not friendly at all. They held guns and the guns were aimed at us.

I recognized the one on the right. He was the guy who'd handed me the professional shellacking on the street the night before. His partner must have been the one holding me. Now they were back for more.

Stomper, Carl and I looked back at Leon simultaneously. The smiles had all left Leon's round face. His eyes held the life and feeling of shiny black marbles. His right fist was filled with a heavy .45 automatic that was leveled at all of us but on me in particular.

"It makes sense now," I said softly. "We're the only ones besides you who know that Stomper is back, right, Leon? Except for Isaac, that is."

"That young buck will be easy enough to nail," said Leon with no emotion whatsoever.

Stomper Crawford half rose from his chair. His fists were clenched into angry knots.

"If you touch a hand to that boy, Leon, so help me I'll—"

The words seemed to be cut off and forced back down his throat as Leon shifted the .45 slightly.

"You'll do nothing, Stomp," Leon told him. "You'll be dead. I knew you didn't recognize me when you saw me cut that dude in the alley that night. But a thing like that implants itself in a man's mind. He thinks about it for the rest of his life. Someday you might see something about me, some way I moved, anything, and it would make you think of that killer in that alley. I just couldn't wait for that to happen, Stomp. The people I run things for don't like complications."

Next to me, Carl Hensman's face was fish belly white.

There was no excitement in his voice now, only quavering fear.

"What the hell's going to happen to us?" he asked anyone who would answer.

"Leon's going to wipe the slate clean," I told him. "As far as anyone else is concerned, Stomper Crawford is still missing. He never came back. Who was that guy you killed, Leon? Some rival pusher?"

"Something like that. The people I work for call it making your bones. I had to waste the dude if I wanted my own concession. It was worth it, O'Dair. I've got a nice profitable operation here. Any high the customer wants for a price."

"And I thought I knew my way around uptown."

"It's too bad you had to stick your nose in," he said. "I sent my boys out last night to, uh, persuade you to let things be. But you always were a stubborn son. Now I've got to waste you, too."

He said it almost as if he meant it. Then he rose to his feet, snapping his head briefly toward the back door leading out of the place, down beyond the end of the bar. "Let's go. Line up behind each other and move it very slow."

They could have killed us there and they might have, had it been night. But gunfire would travel on a lazy Sunday afternoon and might draw too many questions and too many cops. Even at this end of town.

We filed toward the door as we were told. There was nothing else we could do. Except to watch for a break and when it came, to grab it.

Carl would be next to useless in any action that went down, that was obvious. He was between Stomper and me, practically in shock. From behind, I could see that Stomper was walking with a sort of wound-up tenseness, that he was waiting for a break too. But we were facing three guns, and you always have to be careful around guns.

Then we were stepping into the sunshine again, this time into the alley behind *Leon's* where it had all begun. A shiny Lincoln stood waiting silently. Everything was quiet except for our footfalls on the pavement. The city could have been a million miles away beyond the walls of the alley.

Leon motioned again.

"Get in and don't waste time or I start blowing off knee-caps," he said and his eyes said that he meant it.

And that's when the break came.

It was more of a blitzkrieg than a break. A kaleidoscope of movement. Flashes of descending commando-like out-fits. Black. Black on black. The cries of an attacking army. Rushing, moving. They came from the roofs on both sides of the alley. At least ten of them but it seemed like more, they were so fast. They sailed into the men with the guns and everything changed. Suddenly, it was a free-for-all.

I saw Isaac Crawford, lithe and angry as ever, taking care of the big dude who had pounded me last night. Isaac was half the guy's weight, but a few finely executed Kung Fu moves sent the big man spinning into a brick wall.

There was more at the other end of the alley. Isaac Crawford's Neighborhood Action Group may have been the cavalry to the rescue, but the scene wasn't secured just yet.

The other of Leon's two helpers was putting up a mighty struggle and it looked as if he might make it out of the alley. But he'd dropped his gun. I saw Stomper lean over and pick it up, work his way around behind the guy and brain him with it, hard, and that was that.

Leaving my attention free for Leon, the rat I'd always considered a friend. Some of Isaac's pals had almost had him down but foul knee kicks had cleared them away. Now he was aiming through the crowd at the other end of the alley, and I knew without checking that the .45 was drawing a bead on the back of Stomper Crawford's head.

I sailed into Leon with a low tackle, my left pushing his gun up while my right and the body behind it and the force of the tackle sent him pitching down with me. The .45 blasted into the air over my head, instantly followed by the sound, almost as loud, of Leon's head smacking the pavement. A very satisfying sound. Then he was still.

I leaned back on my haunches, caught my breath and looked down at him. He wasn't dead, but he wasn't going anywhere. He was out cold.

A friendly arm helped me to my feet. It was Isaac. Stomper and Carl stood beside him. In the background, the young men of Isaac's Neighborhood Action Group were keeping a tight ring around the other two. They weren't going anywhere, either.

Sirens were approaching from the distance, beyond the canyon walls of the alley. I looked at Isaac.

"Thanks for keeping that part of the bargain," I said. "You didn't have to call the police."

"You didn't have to use yourself as bait. But did you think things were going to break this fast?"

I shook my head.

"Leon caught me napping," I admitted. "But it fits now. Stomper had trouble finding him in the club that night after the kill. The reason was that Leon was coming in via the front door from the alley. This afternoon we thought he was setting up a jam session, but the only people he called were his two thugs."

Stomper Crawford had regained most of his composure. He didn't look like a man who'd just been skull busting in an alley. He had regained his quiet, basic dignity, too.

"Would anyone mind explaining what just went down here?" he asked.

The question was directed at both of us, but Isaac fielded it.

"O'Dair found me this afternoon while you were at Carl's," he said. "He rapped some sense into my fool head. He convinced me that we could work together. He was your bodyguard but he's white and he knew that wouldn't stop anybody on this end of town. It wasn't supposed to.

"The guys in the Group and I have been keeping back, following you since you left Carl's, Dad. You had enough on your mind without worrying about security. Even that rift last night helped. It gave me a reason for not being on the scene. O'Dair thought that might help things to happen. I guess it did."

Stomper Crawford looked at me then and all of the weariness was gone. His eyes burned with the same spark that had illuminated those old publicity photos back when he'd been King of the Blues. Only there was something else now, too, and I think it was for me.

I think it was respect.

"It doesn't sound like you were napping at all, O'Dair," he said. "I want to thank both you and my son for saving my life."

Then he turned the look on Isaac. The close father-son bond was still there. But now there was the respect of one *man* for another, and that meant a lot to both of them . . .

Carl Hensman finally broke the spell. He was still pale, but recovering fast.

"Well, uh, now that that Leon's out of the way," he said, almost as if there weren't converging cops and bruised bodies all over the place, "do ya think we can start making plans for a real jam session? Stomper, I think we ought to—"

I interrupted with a laugh that wouldn't stay down.

"Stomper," I said, "you stick with these guys, hear? Isaac is right about not trusting anybody. With an attitude like that he'll make you a fine agent. And a producer with a one-track mind never hurt anybody."

"I believe you're right," Stomper nodded sagely, looking from his son to his number one fan. "I believe these boys could make old Stomper a blues king all over again."

And he was right.

That's exactly what they did.

ABOUT THE AUTHOR

Stephen Mertz has written in numerous genres under a variety of pseudonyms. His novels have been widely translated and have sold millions of copies worldwide. He lives in the Southwest, and is presently hard at work on a new book.